WORDS OF STONE

"Henkes's craftsmanship [demonstrates] rich characterization, dramatic subplots, and striking visual images . . . The author's respect for the complexity of young people's lives is apparent in this outstanding novel."

—*School Library Journal*, starred review

"What readers will love about this book is the friendship betw⋯⋯eir mee⋯⋯

⋯*ist*

"Th⋯⋯n-
shi⋯⋯

ks

Paperback Hen

Henkes, Kevin
Words of Stone
RL 5.0   5 pts.   Quiz #6400

KEVIN HENKES

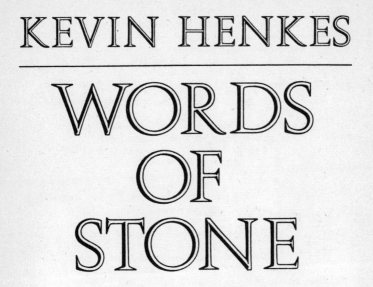

WORDS
OF
STONE

PUFFIN BOOKS

PUFFIN BOOKS
Published by the Penguin Group
Penguin Books USA Inc., 375 Hudson Street, New York, New York 10014, U.S.A.
Penguin Books Ltd, 27 Wrights Lane, London W8 5TZ, England
Penguin Books Australia Ltd, Ringwood, Victoria, Australia
Penguin Books Canada Ltd, 10 Alcorn Avenue, Toronto, Ontario, Canada M4V 3B2
Penguin Books (N.Z.) Ltd, 182–190 Wairau Road, Auckland 10, New Zealand

Penguin Books Ltd, Registered Offices: Harmondsworth, Middlesex, England

First published in the United States of America by Greenwillow Books,
a division of William Morrow and Company, Inc., 1992
Reprinted by arrangement with William Morrow and Company, Inc.
Published in Puffin Books, 1993

1 3 5 7 9 10 8 6 4 2

LIBRARY OF CONGRESS CATALOGING-IN-PUBLICATION DATA
Henkes, Kevin.
Words of stone / Kevin Henkes.   p.   cm.
"First published in the United States of America by Greenwillow
Books, a division of William Morrow and Company, Inc., 1992"—T.p. verso.
Summary: Busy trying to deal with his many fears and his troubled
feelings for his dead mother, ten-year-old Blaze has his life
changed when he meets the boisterous and irresistible Joselle.
ISBN 0-14-036601-6
[1. Friendship—Fiction.   2. Mother and child—Fiction.   3. Fear—
Fiction.]   I. Title.
[PZ7.H389Wo   1993]   [Fic]—dc20   93-7488   CIP   AC
Printed in the United States of America

For Laura and Susan,
with thanks to Gretchen, Tom, Jen, K.T., and Altie

CONTENTS

BLAZE

Blaze Werla buried Ortman before breakfast. It was the fifth of July, and already the day was white hot. Blaze peeled off his T-shirt and tossed it on the hard ground. He shoveled quickly and furtively, making a small, neat hole the size of a basketball. When the digging was through, Blaze knelt, and using both arms and cupped hands, filled the hole back up, covering Ortman forever. There was something fierce about the manner in which Blaze worked—the determined line of his mouth, the tension that rippled across his back. Dirt stuck to Blaze's sweaty body like bread crumbs; his damp red hair clung to his forehead in ringlets. Blaze slapped the ground flat with the palms of his hands, making a thudding sound and remembering all the other burials, glancing at the nearby stones that marked them.

Burials. There had been four others before Ortman. (Not counting his mother's.) The small graves formed a partial ring around the huge black locust tree on the hill near the highway behind Blaze's house. First there had been Benny. Then Ajax. Next Ken. Then Harold. And now Ortman. Blaze wondered what he would do once the circle was complete. Where would he bury then? He was ten years old. Would he still need to do this when he was twelve? Fifteen? He hoped not. He was tired of being afraid.

Blaze stood and stamped the dirt over Ortman one last time. He picked up the stone he had chosen earlier that morning and held it for a few seconds, as if it were a large egg containing precious life. He had chosen the stone because of its markings: pale mossy blotches that looked like bull's-eyes. Blaze set the stone down firmly in place. "Goodbye, Ortman," he whispered. Blaze backed up, scratched the scars on his ankles with either foot, ran his dirty hand through his hair, and stared at the grave site until the crescent of stones blurred before him, becoming a broken pearl bracelet around the arm of a tree it bound.

□   □   □

On the way down the hill toward home, Blaze was already creating someone new in his mind to take Ortman's place. Someone who would be big. Someone who would be tall. Someone who would be fearless. Someone who would be everything Blaze was not.

2

Blaze was slight, with small feet and hands. He thought his fingers resembled birthday candles, especially compared to his father's ample, knuckly ones. At school, Blaze was the shortest student in his class. His identity with many kids from other grades hinged solely upon his size and his red hair. His hair was so distinctive, in fact, that passersby often turned their heads to take notice. His clear blue eyes had a similar effect on people. Freckles peppered Blaze's cheeks and the bridge of his nose. His eyelashes were full and as transparent as fishing line. And—he was fearful.

Blaze swatted at the leafy, waist-high weeds that surrounded him and thought, I am a contradiction—my name is Blaze and I'm afraid of fire. And fire was only the beginning of a long list of things that made Blaze's head prickle just thinking of them.

Fire. Large dogs. Wasps. The dark.

And then there were the other things. The more important things. The really frightening ones. Nightmares. The Ferris wheel at the fairgrounds. The Fourth of July.

Blaze fixed his attention on the drooping slate roof of his house in the near distance. "Come on . . . *Simon*," he said over his shoulder into the warm breeze. "Let's go eat."

□   □   □

"Morning, Blaze," Nova called pleasantly when she heard the screen door open and gently close.

"Morning, Grandma," Blaze said, entering the

kitchen. He walked to the sink and began washing his hands methodically with liquid dish soap, making a thick lather that worked its way up his arms. *Ortman's dead,* he said matter-of-factly in his head, watching a tiny pink-ish blue bubble rise from his hands. *Now I've got Simon.*

Blaze didn't believe in imaginary friends the way he truly had when he was younger. He didn't set places for them at the table or make himself as small as possible in bed to leave room for them. He didn't talk to them out loud when anyone might hear. But every July he formed a new one. It was habit as much as anything else.

In a way, he compared it to Nova's practice of saying "Rabbit, rabbit, rabbit" for good luck on the first day of each month. It had to be her first words spoken or else it didn't work. Nova was far from superstitious, and yet, if she forgot to say it, she seemed annoyed with herself all morning.

Blaze also compared it to the relationship his father had with God. Although he had told Blaze many times that he didn't really know what he believed, Glenn said that he prayed every now and then. He talked to God when no one else was around.

Glenn had his version of God. Nova had "Rabbit, rab-bit, rabbit." And Blaze had Simon.

"Well, what can I get you for breakfast?" Nova asked mildly.

Blaze had been looking out the window toward the hill. He turned and faced his grandmother. "Scrambled eggs, please," he said. And Nova hummed while she

4

made them. At the stove, with her back to Blaze, Nova's wispy moth-colored hair looked just like a dandelion right before you make a wish and blow it. But nothing else about Nova was wispy. She was generous in both size and spirit.

Breakfast was Blaze's favorite meal of the day, and the kitchen was his favorite room in the house. Towels, pots, pans, and various other cooking utensils hung on hooks from the walls and ceiling, reminding Blaze of the buy-and-sell shop in town. Four wide windows let in enough sunlight to balance the clutter. In the early morning, the dramatic shadows of the suspended spatulas and ladles spilled down the flowered wallpaper like stalactites. Or were they stalagmites? Blaze could never keep them straight. He had confused them on his final science test of the school year only last month.

During the summer, Blaze always ate breakfast with Nova, just the two of them at the thick, round oak table. Nova unerringly sensed Blaze's moods; she knew when he wanted to talk and when quiet seemed to be what was needed. If Nova wasn't asking Blaze questions or maintaining a peaceful, necessary silence, she was humming (as she was now); that meant she was deep in thought. Blaze was certain that Nova's low murmuring that morning was due to the cucumber beetles she had been battling in her squash patch. Books and magazines on organic gardening were stacked on the counter by the sink like dirty dishes.

Humming. Then silence. Then only the sound of silverware playing against china.

"I don't know how you do it—getting up at this hour when you don't have to," Glenn said, suddenly appearing in the kitchen doorway.

"Hi, Dad," Blaze said with a start, surprised by Glenn's unusually early jump on the day. His eyes skated up to meet his father's. Ordinarily breakfast was long finished by the time Glenn made it out of bed.

"Morning, Glenn. Eggs today?" Nova asked.

"Just coffee." He padded barefooted across the cracking linoleum and reached for a mug from the cupboard. Glenn was tall and big-boned. His straight blond hair fell into his eyes and barely grazed his shoulders, hiding the ringed birthmark on the back of his neck. It was purple and looked like Saturn. When Blaze was mad at his father, he pretended that the birthmark meant that Glenn was really an alien from outer space. "So what's on the agenda for you two today?" Glenn asked, filling his mug. He sat at the table precisely halfway between Blaze and Nova.

"Cucumber beetles," Nova said. "I'm going to try to lick them with a mixture of vanilla and water. It's a trick I read about in one of my magazines," she added, working her fingers as if she held a spray bottle.

"And you?" Glenn said, looking at Blaze.

Blaze shrugged. "Nothing really."

Glenn rubbed his steel gray eyes and yawned, his wide

6

unshaven jaw opening and closing like a machine. "Want a ride into town? You could call someone from school."

"Nah," Blaze replied, wrinkling his nose and shaking his head.

"I'll take you to the lake or the park. Anywhere you want to go."

"The moon?" Blaze joked.

Glenn yawned and chuckled at the same time.

"I think I'll just mess around here," Blaze told him.

After rubbing his eyes again, Glenn massaged the space between his eyebrows. "Just don't think too much," he said slowly, turning his mug on the table and winking. "It's not good for you." He rose with his coffee and headed toward the back door. He stopped at the sink and leaned against it momentarily. "Oh, by the way . . ." he said. He thrust his hand deep into his pocket and pulled out something small. He flung it gently across the tabletop. It was an old rusty skeleton key. It stopped right beside Blaze's plate, kissing his fork. "I found it yesterday," Glenn said. "For your collection."

"Thanks," Blaze answered. He watched Glenn disappear down the hallway, the key floating on the fringe of his vision. His ankles itched. Blaze knew that Glenn wouldn't give him keys if he knew why he saved them.

But here was a new one. Right before him. An ancient thing. It might be my best one yet, Blaze thought. The key's sharp metallic scent tickled Blaze's nostrils. He scooped it up and fingered it, and it seemed to burn in his hand. Blaze wondered who it had once belonged to, what lock it would release, whose door it might open.

□   □   □

It would be a typical July day. Glenn would spend it in the sagging garage that he had converted into a studio, emerging at dinnertime flecked with paint of all colors. Then he'd return and work again until very late, maybe until dawn. Unlike most fathers, Glenn was home all day in the summer. He was a high-school art teacher who devoted his entire vacation to painting large canvases that Blaze liked, but didn't quite understand. Nova would bustle about the kitchen and her garden—concocting, canning, weeding, pruning, and trying to exterminate cucumber beetles for all time. And Blaze would wander throughout the house and around the hill, occasionally talking to someone that no one else could see.

And it would be a typical July night for Blaze. In bed, he would will himself not to dream. Or, at least, not to remember his dreams when he awoke. He would take the library book from his nightstand, open it halfway, and place it beside him to look as if he had been reading. His mason jar filled with his lost key collection would be on the floor within reach. Then, his lamp still on, Blaze would settle in among his nest of four pillows, wishing and waiting for morning light.

BLAZE

When Blaze woke up the next morning his chest ached with strangeness. He had been dreaming. It was a dream he had had before. In it a maze of black snakes burst into flames at his feet while he struggled to open a door. The door was held tightly closed by a series of locks. His mother's voice came from behind the door. Sometimes in the dream he would have a key. But even when he did, it would never work.

Don't think about it, Blaze told himself.

His dreams were always so vivid during the summer. He might not remember having a dream for months, but come July they would return. It was peculiar the way that worked.

Blaze blinked and looked around. His room focused about him, becoming familiar and touchable. The library book from the night before was now closed and neatly placed on his nightstand, his bedside lamp turned off. Although he had never actually seen Nova or Glenn do these things, he had often sensed a presence—passing as a shadow, removing the book, turning off the light, tugging the bedclothes up under his chin, touching his forehead, pulling the door closed.

Blaze sat up and swung his legs out from under the sheet. It was dawn. A gust of wind caused the loose window screen to flutter and the faded plaid curtains to balloon and collapse. The curtains had worn thin in many places and were at least as old as Blaze. So was the large, multicolored oval rug that covered most of the floor. But nearly everything else was relatively new in comparison. The bookshelf, the bed, the nightstand, the dresser. Blaze could still remember the old blue-striped wallpaper, but now the walls were white. He had picked the paint himself. Snowflake, it was called on the paint chart.

It was several summers earlier that Glenn had urged Blaze to redecorate his room. "I could paint the solar system on your ceiling," Glenn had suggested. "And we could buy some of those neat glow-in-the-dark stars to stick on." Glenn paused, tapping his fingers on his chin. "We could redo the walls, too. This wallpaper's not the greatest. We'd have to clean this place out first, though. Get rid of some of this old baby stuff." As he spoke,

10

Glenn gestured vaguely toward the toys, knickknacks, and books that crowded Blaze's shelves, drawers, closet, and the dusty space under his bed. Things he had long outgrown. "What do you think?"

Blaze was looking at his prized possession—a plastic Noah's ark replica—perched atop the low overstuffed bookcase. "Okay," he answered reluctantly, not wanting to disappoint Glenn.

"Great!"

"But can I keep my ark?" Blaze's voice was urgent.

Glenn hugged him. "Of course," he said into his son's red hair.

Blaze picked the ark off the shelf and clutched it tightly. "And can we just paint the walls and ceiling white? No solar system?"

"You bet," said Glenn.

Blaze figured that the lighter the walls and ceiling were, the lighter his room would be at night.

Blaze still had the ark. He kept it tucked safely under his bed. Out of sight if a friend from school came over. Now he pulled it out and brought it to the window. Resting one end of it on the sill, he held it in place with his stomach and drew open the curtains to glance at the hill. He did this every morning. But that morning there was something different. Something very strange. Something so strange that Blaze stepped back from the window in surprise, causing his ark to fall. It cracked in half at his feet, little animals scattering across the floor like the pieces of a shattered glass.

◻   ◻   ◻

A chill hit Blaze in the small of his back and spread to his neck. Written with stones on the broad, mowed stretch of the hillside was the word REENA. Blaze felt hazy and anxious. His heart rattled. He closed his eyes and counted to ten before opening them again. Nothing had changed. Squinting, Blaze leaned on the windowsill, his nose pressed to the screen, then pulled back. The word was still there. It seemed to fill the window. The window seemed to fill the room. Blaze was smaller than ever.

REENA.

"Who did this, Simon?" Blaze whispered. His first thought was to wake Glenn, but something deep and in-stinctive led him in another direction. Temporarily for-getting about his ark, Blaze slipped into some shorts, a T-shirt, and shoes. His hands shook, fumbling with his laces and getting tangled in the folds of his shirt. But, once dressed, he managed to move quickly and quietly so as not to wake anyone—melting down the stairs, tip-toeing throughout the house, and then pushing up the hill with all his might.

When Blaze stopped, he was gasping for air. He dou-bled over—hands on knees—and tried to breathe evenly. His breath felt warm on his skin. He lifted his head. The letters were enormous up so close. Impul-sively, Blaze shoved stone after stone aside with his feet,

12

scrambling them so no one else could read the word. A few he heaved with his hands; they tumbled down the slope. A round and smooth stone with green rings on it caught his attention. It looked exactly like the stone he had chosen to mark Ortman's grave. He examined it closely. Recognized it.

"Oh, no," Blaze said, stunned all over again. The sky and the grass changed places in his vision as he raced for the black locust tree. After stumbling twice, he used his hands in an animal-like fashion to help him move without falling.

He wanted to cry. His stones were missing. All five of them. Whoever had written REENA had used them to help construct the letters. Blaze circled the tree a number of times, raising a cloud of dust. Then he sat resting against it, thinking. Waiting. Without the slightest idea of what to do next. A group of crows swooped down nearby. They strutted in a chaotic formation, their calls long and raucous. In a sudden beating of glossy black wings, they took off again. Up, up, up they flew, and Blaze watched, feeling as if he were sinking.

3

BLAZE

Blaze spent the morning in his bedroom, feeling un-connected. He was fixing his ark with Elmer's Glue. While he waited for the glue to dry, he gathered the small animals he had dropped earlier and played with them—first grouping them by color, then lining them up in a row. He held a memory of doing this with his mother, Reena. He remembered placing the pairs of ani-mals—elephants, giraffes, bears, sheep—on one of the inner braided coils of the rug in his room, following the rug's contour, curving the line of the procession until it formed an oval. Reena and Blaze in the middle. Now there was only one of each plastic animal. When Blaze was five and Reena died, he took one animal from each pair and smashed them with a brick behind the house. Because the ark was his favorite toy and he wanted to punish himself somehow. Because a pair of anything didn't seem right.

Periodically, Blaze peered out the window, turning his gaze from left to right, checking for another message in stone. He was continually relieved when he found only the remains of the first, still strewn haphazardly across the hill like popcorn on a theater floor. Who did it? He kept asking himself that question. And he kept coming up with no answer. Although Blaze knew in his heart that neither Nova nor Glenn had done it, he toyed with the possibility.

Nova. She rarely left the house or garden, except to go grocery shopping. It was unusual for her to complain, but Blaze knew that by the end of the day her thick legs were puffy and sore. She often had to elevate them with pillows. Once, she said she had the legs of a ninety-year-old woman, even though she was only sixty. Her legs reminded Blaze of maps—bumpy blue veins connecting feet to knees like crooked highways. When he was younger, Blaze had found comfort in running his fingers over the bulging veins. Compared to them, the scars on his ankles seemed insignificant. The pinkish skin on his ankles was rippled, as if tiny worms were trapped underneath. It was as if twisting snakes were trapped under Nova's skin. Her legs didn't stop her from cooking and gardening with a passion, but trudging up the hill and

rolling stones around to spell the name of her dead
daughter was surely the last thing she would do.

And Glenn? It wasn't his style. Glenn was a private
person. And anyway, it was hard enough to coax him
from his studio for dinner or a telephone call on a summer day. Blaze knew he wouldn't take time away from
his painting to do something like this.

Who then?

Not his classmates. None of them lived this far out in
the country. (Blaze was the first one picked up and the
last one dropped off by the bus each school day.) And
although Blaze didn't have a best friend, he was treated
with genuine fondness by students and teachers alike.
He was smart, but not the smartest. Shy, but not the
most shy. He was ninth fastest in his class. And he was
considered by some to be the best artist in the entire
school. He could draw nearly any popular cartoon char-
acter upon request.

There were only two fellow classmates that Blaze
didn't like—Teddy Burman and Chelsea Kurz—but they
both liked him, so they were out of the question. Teddy
was a tiresome braggart and Chelsea was a tireless
brown-noser.

At Alan B. Shepard Elementary, Blaze was often
called Big Red (a nickname that didn't bother him at
all), even by Mr. Wiebe, the principal, who'd always try
to ruffle Blaze's hair if he spotted him among the noisy
throng that paraded past his office on the way to and
from recess.

Floy Stark was a possibility, but a vague one. She lived alone on the other side of the hill in a tidy, boxlike house the color of celery. She was about Nova's age, maybe younger. Sometimes Blaze lay on the hill and watched the Stark house. Nothing interesting ever happened. Floy did ordinary things like hang laundry on the clothesline, wash windows, cut the grass, and play fetch with a terrifying German shepherd she called Gary (who was, thank goodness, usually chained safely to the garage). That was about it.

Blaze couldn't think of anyone else. "Help me, Simon," Blaze said, flopping onto his bed like a fish. Pressed into his hand was a tiny plastic bird, wings outstretched, anticipating flight. He lay on his back, staring at the ceiling, trying to weave a plan. And remembering.

□　　□　　□

Soon after Reena died, Blaze, Nova, and Glenn went to a therapist together. Blaze couldn't remember how many sessions they had gone to, but he would never forget how uncomfortable he felt at them. "She looks at me like I'm an ant on a stick," Blaze told Glenn and Nova meekly, after what turned out to be their last session. They were walking across the parking lot toward their car. Blaze inhaled deeply, so happy to be out of Dr. Zondag's office. He sniffed his sleeve; the lemony smell of the office still lingered and he waved his shirttail in the air.

Glenn and Nova shared a long glance.

"It's really important to talk about things, you know," Glenn said cautiously, leaning against the car, jingling his keys.

Blaze nodded. He waited for Glenn to unlock the door, then crawled into the backseat. The late afternoon sun spilled into the car, creating sharp-edged shadows. Blaze moved his hand in and out of the warm light.

They stopped at a drive-in restaurant on the way home. Before they ordered, Glenn turned in his seat and leaned over toward Blaze. His head was touching the roof of the car, pulling his hair to one side as if he had slept on it funny. "We don't have to go back," Glenn said slowly. "But you have to promise that you'll always ask me anything you want to. Even if you think it's silly or stupid. I want you to always be able to talk to me." Glenn ran his hand along the back of Blaze's neck and rested it on his shoulder. "Mom would want it that way."

Semis and cars rolled by on the highway while they had dinner. Blaze ate nearly half of his hamburger and he almost finished his junior chocolate shake—something he had never done before. He slurped his shake so quickly he got a headache. The pain thrilled him and he tried it again, egged on by his sense of relief.

As they pulled out of the driveway and threaded into the stream of traffic to go home, Glenn said, "Nothing's too big or too small to tell me or ask me. You know that."

◻   ◻   ◻

Blaze *did* know that. And yet he couldn't bring himself to tell Glenn about what he had seen on the hill that
morning. For several reasons.

First, he was beginning to wonder if he had only imagined it or dreamed it. (That's what he wanted to think.)

Second, if it hadn't been a dream, would Glenn believe him anyway? Considering that Blaze had already
jumbled the stones so that the hill looked as it always
did?

Third, he was still shy when it came to talking about
Reena with Glenn sometimes, even though he knew that
he shouldn't be. Sometimes his unspoken words were almost tangible, he was so close to talking. Sometimes he
stopped himself because he didn't want to take a chance
on making Glenn sad. Blaze had seen Glenn cry once
when Reena was ill. It had made Blaze feel as small as
a dot and completely afraid. Now and then Blaze heard
Glenn and Nova talk about Reena in what Blaze thought
were sad, hushed voices. Of course, Glenn said things
about Reena to Blaze, remembered things with him, but
Glenn always initiated the conversations. That was the
difference. Blaze didn't want to ask or say something
about Reena if he couldn't be absolutely certain that the
time was perfect and that Glenn would want to talk
about her. Even at school if Blaze didn't understand
something, he'd often try to figure it out by himself
rather than raise his hand and ask a question.

And then there was the other reason. The eerie thought he was trying to suppress. The thought that his mother was somehow responsible for writing her name on the hill outside his bedroom window.

It was then that Blaze decided to handle this thing on his own. (With Simon, of course.) Maybe he hadn't been able to ride the Ferris wheel on the Fourth of July. Again. But this was surely a way to prove his bravery. He would get to the bottom of this. Blaze didn't want to be afraid anymore.

4

JOSELLE

Joselle Stark dried her eyes with the back of her hand. "No, I'm *not* crying," she called fiercely. She was crouched on the ivory wicker clothes hamper in her grandmother's narrow bathroom. She wound her arms tightly around her knees and rocked back and forth. The hamper creaked and sagged in rhythm.

"Joselle? What are you doing in there?"

"I'm coming, Grammy!" Joselle scooted down and looked at herself in the mirror on the back of the door. I'm a mess, she thought, sniffling. Her dark brown hair hung in tangled strands around her face, one untamed clump falling over her right eye. "I wish my hair would cover my *mouth*," she muttered, flipping her hair back.

Joselle's teeth were perfectly shaped, but they were sizes too big for her mouth. In fact, her teeth were so big, it took a conscious effort on Joselle's part to keep her mouth closed. Piano keys, she called them. And she had the nervous habit of bringing her hand up to her mouth, pretending to play a tune on her teeth, humming as she did.

Joselle wasn't fat, but her knees and elbows were dimpled like a baby's, and her arms and legs looked meaty. She was wearing an extra-large raspberry sweatshirt with the sleeves cut off; it hung to her thighs. The circles under her eyes matched her clothing in color. Joselle knew that her grandmother's eyesight wasn't terrific, but she knew that her grandmother wasn't blind, either. She hoped her grandmother wouldn't be able to tell that her eyes were bloodshot. Joselle stuck her tongue out at herself in the mirror. She flushed the toilet for effect, unlocked the door, and marched into the hallway, her red rubber thongs slapping crisply against her feet.

"What were you doing in there, sweetie?" Floy asked.

"Grammy, you're old enough to know what goes on in a bathroom," Joselle replied, walking away, an agonized look on her face.

"I'm also old enough to know when someone's been crying." Floy grabbed Joselle by the shoulders and spun her around. Floy was strong, despite her petite size, her grip unflinching. "You *were* crying." She drew Joselle against her chest. They were so close, Joselle could feel two heartbeats.

22

Joselle started to cry again. "I hate and despise my mother," she sobbed into her grandmother's sleeveless lavender shift.

"I know, I know," Floy soothed. "Come to the sofa. Let me do your eyelids."

Floy settled into the low end of the worn velour sofa and Joselle lay down, her head on her grandmother's lap, her eyes closed firmly. Although their visits were seldom and sporadic, the instant Floy touched Joselle's eyelids it was as if they had never been apart. "I've done this for you since you were a baby," Floy said.

"Since forever," Joselle whispered.

"Relax," Floy said, as she gently stroked Joselle's eyelids over and over. "Your eyelids are the color of my needlepoint lilacs."

Joselle couldn't have cared less about lilacs. Or needlepoint. Her mother had abandoned her. The Beautiful Vicki had taken off with her boyfriend Rick to "get away to try to be happy for a while without any interruptions." The more Joselle thought about it, the more upset she became. Her body shook; tears slid down her cheeks.

Her mother had done stupid, impulsive things before, but this was by far the worst. And the stupid, impulsive things usually had to do with men. Life would be going along just fine until The Beautiful Vicki became interested in someone new. As her interest escalated, so would her time away from Joselle and so would her rash behavior. Before Rick, Vicki had been involved with a man named Bert. This was late last summer. Bert had come into the restaurant where Vicki worked and charmed her completely. Bert was all she could talk about. It wasn't long before he moved in.

Before Bert, Vicki and Joselle had watched "The Mary Tyler Moore Show" in reruns every weekday night after the ten o'clock news. Since it was summer, Vicki didn't mind if Joselle stayed up so late. It became ritual. Every night "Mary Tyler Moore." Every night cream soda. Every night microwave popcorn sprinkled with Parmesan cheese. Every night Vicki and Joselle sprawled on the futon, the little electric fan turning side to side, cooling them off as they licked their cheesy fingers clean and laughed at Mary Richards and Rhoda Morgenstern. Every night the hypnotic light of the television flashing across the walls of the dark, dark room like a fire in a cave.

"This is my all-time favorite show," Vicki would say.

"We could watch it all night," Joselle would add, scooching closer to her mother. "If it was on all night."

But as soon as Bert came, everything changed. No more "Mary Tyler Moore" (he preferred "M*A*S*H" and Vicki let him watch it). No more microwave popcorn with Parmesan cheese and cream soda alone with Vicki. No more comfortable routine.

"He helps pay for the groceries and the electric bills," Vicki would tell Joselle. "And besides, he makes me happy."

"He doesn't make *me* happy," Joselle would counter. "And you hardly spend any time with me anymore."

"I've spent more time with you than with anyone—nearly my whole life."

"What about 'Mary Tyler Moore'? You even said it was your favorite show."

"So I changed my mind." Vicki sighed, exhaling frustration, losing patience quickly. "'M*A*S*H' is real. Watch it—you might learn something."

Joselle was ecstatic when Bert finally moved out about four months later. In a matter of weeks, things settled back to the way they had been, and Joselle and Vicki's spats were few and far between. But then Rick entered their lives, and the cycle began repeating itself.

A small part of Joselle seemed to understand what made Vicki change from being the mother she loved to being the mother she didn't. But she was always unprepared when it happened. Joselle brought her hand up to her mouth and began playing "Strangers in the Night" on her teeth.

"Listen, it won't be so bad," Floy said, competing with the melody. "I'm sure your mother will be back soon. You'll like it here. And anyway, it could be worse—that little Werla boy from around the hill doesn't even *have* a mother."

Suddenly Joselle stopped humming and crying and trembling. She sat up and stared at Floy with great astonished eyes. "You mean that skinny redhead I saw sitting on the hill this morning doesn't have a mother."

Floy nodded.

"Tell me, tell me," Joselle demanded, snatching her

grandmother's hands and squeezing them like sponges. She hoped that the skinny redhead's life story would be worse than hers. She hoped that it would be absolutely dreadful.

◻   ◻   ◻

Joselle listened hungrily. She hung on Floy's every word until even the smallest incident blossomed into full tragedy in her mind. And there was tragedy enough, with or without the aid of Joselle's imagination.

The boy's name was Blaze Werla. And his mother had died when he was just five years old. Of cancer. "Her name was Reena," Floy said, doing Joselle's eyelids again. "She was so young."

Reena. Joselle liked the sound of the name. She thought it was kind of exotic and sexy. She repeated it softly, drawing out the long E sound like a bird call. *Reeeeena.*

"She died in the middle of the summer," Floy continued, "when it was hot and muggy. She had long, thick red hair, and I remember thinking how sad it was when she lost it."

"Lost her hair?" Joselle said, her eyes widening.

"From the treatment. Chemotherapy, it's called," Floy explained. "It made her hair fall out. She wore pretty scarves then. Bright ones. The last time I saw her, she was resting on a lawn chair in their yard wearing a chartreuse scarf that was knotted at the top of her head."

Joselle imagined the scene: The exotic and sexy Reena was so thin you could practically see every bone in her body. Blaze, her tiny son, was weeping hysterically, picking clumps of her hair off the ground and stuffing them into his pockets. The confused husband (who Joselle knew *nothing* about) was hiding behind a nearby bush staring into space like a lawn ornament.

Floy sighed deeply, regaining Joselle's attention.

"Go on, Grammy," Joselle ordered.

"Oh, sweetie, let's talk about something else. Let's talk about something happy."

"If we did that, I wouldn't have anything to say."

"Oh, Joselle!"

"At least tell me more about the boy," Joselle said in her best supplicating voice.

"Well," Floy said, shrugging, "he's quiet and small and he's about your age. He looks a lot like his mother to me. I remember about a year after Reena died, there was an accident at the fairgrounds. A fire. He burned his legs on the Fourth of July and spent the rest of that summer wrapped in bandages up to his waist. Poor little thing. Of course, he's fine now. I don't really know him, but I see him alone up on the hill a lot. From my window. He must like it up there. So you see," Floy added, "you're not the only one with a complicated life."

"What's that mean? Complicated?"

"Oh, I don't know. Confusing, I guess. Mixed up." Floy took her glasses off and cleaned them in her dress. "But enough of him. Let's talk about you."

27

"No way," Joselle replied quickly, getting up and clapping her hands. She was thinking about the word *complicated*.

"Well, then, why don't we unpack your bags and get your things organized?" Floy suggested cheerfully. "I'm just so glad you're here with me."

Joselle wanted more details (What about the funeral? What about the father? Did he remarry? What did Blaze's legs look like when they were burned? What did they smell like? What did they look like now?), but she figured that she'd work them out of Floy eventually. And the things that Floy wouldn't reveal or had forgotten or didn't know, Joselle would simply have to make up. And they would be the most awful things of all.

5

JOSELLE

Joselle paced about Floy's small house, surveying every corner like a cat. Since she was going to be staying here for a while, she needed to reacquaint herself with the way things looked, smelled, and felt. Joselle moved from room to room, shoving chairs and floor lamps an inch or two in random directions, leaving her mark. She rearranged Floy's Hummel figurines, turning some so that the backs of the children's heads with their odd peaks of hair faced outward.

"Just be careful with those," Floy warned, hovering over Joselle's shoulder, referring to the Hummels. "They're worth money."

Joselle discovered Floy's nail polish, and they took

turns painting each other's fingernails and toenails. Joselle was intrigued by the names of the colors: Rambling Rose, Cherub Frost, Iceberry. She wanted each nail to be a different color, but Floy didn't have that many bottles and some were empty.

"You look racy, Grammy," Joselle said, having a giggle fit.

When their hands and feet had dried, Floy made popcorn and Joselle strung the kernels with a needle and thread, making necklaces. The necklaces reminded Joselle of Hawaiian leis, and the popcorn reminded her of her mother. Joselle laced the garlands around her neck and did a rhythmic hula dance for Floy. Floy found it humorous until Joselle carried the joke to extremes, bumping her rear end into the furniture as part of her dance. Joselle gyrated until she became dizzy, falling into an end table. One of Floy's Hummels—a round-faced girl gazing dreamily at a book—wobbled and nearly fell.

"That's enough," Floy scolded. "And those popcorn necklaces are making grease stains on your shirt."

Joselle blushed with shame. "Leave me alone," she snapped, her eyes pinpoints of anger. She tramped to the front window and rolled herself into the drape. She stared blankly out the window, twizzling a strand of her hair.

After dinner, at the window again, Joselle noticed movement on the hill. It was the red-haired boy. Blaze Werla. Joselle watched him intensely until the window turned blue with the onset of night.

□   □   □

Later, on the sofa that was her bed now, Joselle regretted the meanness that she had shown Floy. At that moment she loved Floy more than anyone. "I'm sorry, Grammy," she whispered into the lonely night. The only one who heard her was Gary, Floy's German shepherd. He trotted over to Joselle from the kitchen, his tail wagging like a wind-up toy. He rested his head on her pillow, and she kissed him between the eyes. After a reciprocal lick, Gary folded himself up into a knobby sack on the floor beside her.

Gary's hairy body and pointy ears made Joselle think of her mother's boyfriend Rick. She wondered where the two of them were. How far they had driven. How long it would take before they wrote or called.

It had only been a few days since The Beautiful Vicki had informed Joselle that she needed a vacation. And Joselle would never forget that fateful day. Joselle had taken a felt-tip marking pen and drawn black stripes along the edges of her teeth to make them look even more like a real piano keyboard. "Look, Vicki," she had said to her mother excitedly. "You know, the black keys." Joselle pointed to her mouth and opened wide to reveal her handiwork.

"God, Joselle," Vicki had replied, throwing down her magazine in exasperation and grabbing Joselle's wrist. "It's things like this that make me—"

Joselle could fill in the blank many ways—crazy, want to send you away forever, regret being a mother.

Vicki pulled Joselle into the bathroom and brushed her teeth for her until her gums bled. "It's not a permanent marker," Joselle tried to explain.

But all Vicki kept saying was, "I could scream. I could just scream!" It was then that Vicki announced that she and Rick were going to take a trip. By themselves.

Joselle stayed in the bathroom, alone, crying, rocking on the toilet. There was greenish gray spittle all over the mirror and on the sink. Joselle knew she would always hate that color. Minty greenish gray.

□   □   □

It wasn't easy getting comfortable on Floy's old sofa with so much to consider. Joselle played her tongue against her teeth and gums and tried to focus on something stupid and safe. The sofa. Joselle imagined that it had been handsome when it was new—red and firm and plush. Now the dye had faded to a dirty wine color. It was soft, but lumpy. And the patchy raised pattern that was supposed to be roses reminded Joselle of bald mutant camels that were more hump than anything else. But soon the pattern resembled the fabric of one of Vicki's skirts. And then it resembled the upholstery in Rick's car. It took a while, but Joselle finally nestled deep into the cushions, wrapped in a thin blue blanket, tight as a parcel. Tomorrow I will show Grammy how much I love her, Joselle thought. And I will complicate the life of Blaze Werla.

6

JOSELLE

"Thank you, Joselle," Floy said, smiling. "That was a wonderful breakfast. Where did you learn to cook so well?"

"Omelets are easy," Joselle said triumphantly, as she wiped the table with a dishcloth. "And I cook a lot at home. If I didn't, I'd starve to death."

Floy leaned back in her chair, saying nothing, the veins in her neck pulsing. The conversation seemed to have ended.

Floy looked older to Joselle that morning, and her face and neck had a bluish cast to them as though her skin had turned translucent and light were shining through. Floy had always been thin, but the older Joselle became, the thinner Floy appeared to be. Almost breakable, like blown glass.

33

"It's true," Joselle said finally. "I *would* starve. Especially since Rick and The Beautiful Vicki took a class at the community college on developing your ESP potential. They lounge around on the futon for hours—which is hardly unusual—and they go into trances to explore other countries. The trances really freak me out. I used to sit and watch them, wondering if they'd be home in time to fix me dinner. Now I just fix it myself. I've gotten good at it." Joselle was playing with crumbs in her hand, and only then did she notice that her hands were still dirty from her secret prebreakfast task. Little crescent moons of dirt shone through the places on Joselle's fingernails where her nail polish had chipped away.

"Well, you can cook for me anytime," Floy said, working at a spot on the tabletop with her thumb.

"I know The Beautiful Vicki's your daughter," Joselle said, glancing at Floy nervously. "And I—" she said, then hesitated a moment, deciding to change the direction in which her comment was headed. "And I was just wondering what I could make you for lunch."

"We've got all morning to decide," Floy said. She rose from the table and reknotted the ties of her bathrobe. "Just tell me one thing—why do you call her The Beautiful Vicki?"

"Because that's her name. And she is."

Floy turned around to face the sink, and her entire body began to move as if small waves rippled under her robe. Joselle was certain that Floy was crying, and her heart dropped as she pulled Floy toward her. But as their eyes met, Joselle's heart became weightless; Floy had been holding back laughter. "The Beautiful Vicki—that takes the cake," Floy managed to say between shrieks. "Well, I always thought she should be a beautician. Lord knows she spends enough money on cosmetics." Floy poked Joselle with her elbow and howled. They pressed together in hysterics.

While Floy went off to shower and dress, Joselle stayed in the kitchen. She opened the silverware drawer and pulled out every teaspoon and tablespoon. She looked at her face in each one. On the back of the spoons, her face was thin and long and right side up. On the other side, her face was wide and upside down. She moved the spoons at varying distances, distorting her face. She was amazed that each time it worked the same—upside down on the inside, right side up on the outside. Vicki had shown her this trick years ago, and Joselle still tested it wherever she went.

Joselle licked a spoon. My mother is smart, she thought.

They had been eating ice cream at the kitchen table right before bed the night that Vicki had presented Joselle with this minor marvel.

"It's magic!" Joselle had said.

"Try another spoon," Vicki suggested.

Joselle tried every spoon in the house, wide-eyed and mystified.

"Does it only work with chocolate ice cream?" Joselle asked.

Vicki opened the refrigerator. "Let's see," she said.

Laughing, they tried jam, cold leftover tomato soup, and maple syrup. They tried milk and orange juice, spooning them out of bowls. They tried peanut butter straight from the jar and sugar right out of the sugar bowl.

"*Every* spoon is magic," Joselle told Vicki, her voice cracking with excitement. "No matter what you're eating with it. Every spoon in the *world*."

They did the dishes together that night, the radio blaring. They played with the suds and serenaded one another using the spoons as pretend microphones. It was after midnight when Vicki finally kissed Joselle goodnight and tucked her in.

"I love being a single girl with you," Vicki whispered.

"Me, too," said Joselle. She had closed her eyes, lulled by Vicki's voice. She was asleep in minutes.

Joselle put the last spoon in its proper place and closed Floy's kitchen drawer. She wondered how her mother could be so perfect sometimes, and other times be as far from perfect as possible.

□   □   □

Joselle was pleased. She had accomplished everything she had set out to do for the entire day, and it wasn't even 9:00 A.M. Not only had she shown Floy how much she loved her by making her breakfast, Joselle had also made Floy laugh harder than she had ever seen anyone laugh. But more importantly, Joselle had done something daring and original. Something that she thought could shake up someone's life. She wasn't exactly sure why she had done it—except she sensed that if she could make someone else more confused than she was, the weight of her own emotions might be lifted. It was worth a try. "Misery loves company," Vicki often said. The idea had begun during the night as a tiny seed that kept growing inside her until she was consumed by it and there was absolutely no way to fight it.

It was amazing how everything had come together so easily. Floy had said that he spent a lot of time on the hill. She knew his mother was dead. And she remembered that there were rocks and stones on the hill. In the weak light before breakfast, Joselle had done something that she hoped would complicate the life of Blaze Werla. She knew that if the situation were reversed, it would surely complicate hers. Joselle giggled with delight. She played the themes from "The Brady Bunch" and "The Mary Tyler Moore Show" on her teeth.

She was in the bathroom with the door locked, sitting on the clothes hamper. When she had finished her tunes, Joselle began decorating her thighs with ball-point-pen tattoos. At first she was going to put them on her arm, but she didn't want anyone to see them. So she settled on her thighs—so far up that they would only be visible if she were naked. And no one ever got a glimpse of her in that condition.

REENA was the first tattoo she gave herself. She was using her four-color pen and chose blue ink, pressing so hard that it hurt. Beneath it, she drew a rose in red ink and a leaf and thorns in green. It looked professional. She admired it. REENA.

This was the second time she had written the word *Reena* that morning. She wanted to write something else with stones on the hillside in a day or two. She practiced on her thighs. In black ink she wrote FIRE! And then in red she wrote YOU'RE ON FIRE, encasing the letters with jagged flames.

Just then Floy pounded on the door. "Joselle, are you upset in there again?" she asked.

Joselle hopped off the hamper, made sure her tattoos were concealed, unlocked the door, and greeted her grandmother holding her pen as if it were a cigarette. "I've never felt better, Grammy," Joselle said, grinning. She waltzed down the hallway blowing pretend smoke haughtily. "By the way," Joselle said, stopping and turning toward Floy, "what do you think is the worst way to die?"

7
BLAZE

The air was dizzy with insects. And Blaze was dizzy under the black locust tree. He had been twirling himself about, his arms outstretched like a propeller, until he was too unsteady to stand. He fell to the ground, and everything continued to whirl.

He had been talking to Simon in his head. About his mother. One piece of information for each full turn. Making a game of it.

She died when I was five and a half. *Turn around.* The last thing we did together was to ride the Ferris wheel at the fairgrounds. *Around.* She was already very sick. *And around.* It's my last memory of her. *Faster.* She was wearing a pink scarf. *Faster.* And there were blue rings under her eyes. *Faster, faster, faster . . . stop.*

Blaze looked straight up. Things were slowing down. He was shielded by a gigantic green canopy that shimmered as the wind blew, throwing shadows across his body. The pieces of sun that filtered through were so bright they hurt his eyes. For a couple of weeks in the spring, the canopy was white and fragrant. And on a clear moonlit night with a breeze, the canopy was silvery, as if made of stars rather than leaves or blossoms. He never thought you could love a tree, but he did. The black locust was perfect—except for the thorns that spun out from the branches like teeth, making it nearly impossible to climb. Blaze took a deep breath. Summer afternoons on the hill smelled of heat and dirt and grass and weeds and laziness. And—lately—of vigilance, caution, suspense. Blaze felt like an alarm clock just waiting to go off.

It had been two days since Reena's name appeared on the hill. Blaze had reconstructed his semicircle of stones around the tree, each marker in its proper place. The other stones he left dotting the hillside here and there. Everything looked exactly as it should, and yet there was a peculiar feeling in the air, as if someone or something strange were lurking nearby. Blaze circled the tree several times, then glided down the hill toward home in a zigzag fashion, his legs scissoring the sunlight.

He waved to Nova, who was bending over in her garden. She stood tall and waved back, calling out his name from beneath her wide-brimmed straw hat. Blaze turned and cut across the lawn, angling toward Glenn's studio.

Blaze often peeked in one of the huge windows to see what his father was working on. He tried to be invisible and quiet, careful not to disturb Glenn.

Glenn painted large canvases crammed with a multitude of figures and objects that were out of proportion in reference to one another. A man might be holding a plum swollen to the size of a basketball, or a woman might be walking a dog that was as large as a horse. Dragonflies and airplanes with the same dimensions flew side by side. Everyone in Glenn's paintings seemed detached, lost in a cool, claustrophobic dreamworld. There was often a red-haired woman in Glenn's paintings; Blaze knew that she was Reena. Sometimes Blaze spotted himself in his father's work—a pale, reedy boy hiding in the background among trees or floating in the air like a cloud. He liked that. It made him feel proud.

At the end of the school year Glenn would build wooden frames and stretch enough canvas to last the summer. Blaze would help. Blaze's favorite part was attaching the canvas to the wooden frames with Glenn's silver staple gun. It was heavy, and Blaze had to concentrate and push hard to get the staples into the frames as deeply as possible. The staple gun had a nasty little kick that jolted Blaze's arm, and it made a whooshing noise that reminded Blaze of getting a vaccination. Sometimes Glenn had to remove the staples and Blaze had to try again. Blaze noticed that it became easier each summer. He was growing stronger.

After the canvases were stretched, they had to be gessoed. Blaze helped with this, too. He had his own brush. Father and son would work together in the hot studio, perspiration beading above their lips like mustaches, first brushing the gesso in one direction, letting it dry, sanding it, then brushing it in the opposite direction, letting it dry, sanding it, brushing again, repeating, repeating, repeating. Canvas after canvas after canvas.

After a couple days of work, the studio was filled with about a dozen taut, white rectangles of various sizes, just waiting to be painted.

"This is either promising and exciting, or scary as hell. It all depends on how you look at it." Glenn would always say something like that as he stared at the empty fields of white laid out flat on the studio floor like perfect rugs. It would often take him a few days to actually begin. And then he would work passionately, as though painting were as important as eating.

Earlier that summer, their annual ritual completed, Glenn gave Blaze one of the canvases. "It's about time you had a real canvas to work on."

Blaze was dumbstruck. He loved to draw and paint, but he usually worked with colored pencils on newsprint tablets, or with watercolors on the back of heavy, dimpled paper that Glenn had done studies on. Most often, he drew television cartoon characters from memory, or he copied panels from comic books. "I don't know what to paint on it," Blaze said. Cartoon characters didn't seem important enough for a real stretched canvas.

"I'll let you use my paints and brushes when you think you're ready," Glenn said. "Do some sketches first."

The canvas was hidden away, leaning against the wall in Blaze's closet. He was waiting for a good idea. Something worthy enough.

Glenn worked in oils, and Blaze liked the way the combination of turpentine, linseed oil, and varnish smelled. When he reached the open window, Blaze inhaled deeply.

He heard laughter and froze. Glenn and a woman Blaze had never seen before were standing face-to-face in front of Glenn's easel. They were both barefooted. The woman had long grayish blond hair that fell to her waist. She was wearing a thick shiny band around her upper arm and an orange sleeveless dress that moved like water in the breeze that swept through the studio. Blaze watched them kiss. He considered closing his eyes, but intensified his gaze instead. Now Glenn stood behind the woman and coiled her hair into a nest on top of her head. He pulled a pencil out from behind his ear and positioned it in the woman's hair so that the bun stayed in place. Blaze had to catch his breath.

❑   ❑   ❑

Glenn had dated other women before. A few—particularly a nurse named Carol—Blaze had liked. She talked openly and comfortably with him, and she gave him small gifts—shells, pens, and candy bars. She wasn't afraid to touch Blaze's arm or lightly rest her hand on his shoulder, but she never hugged or kissed him as if she were trying to be his mother. Carol didn't come around very long, however; maybe two months after Blaze had met her. And Blaze never asked why.

Some of the women Glenn introduced to Blaze made him feel squirmy and shy. They often looked at him with wide pitiful doll's eyes and their voices dripped with a sweetness that said, Oh, you poor motherless boy. His self-consciousness grew in their presence.

Blaze stared at this new woman. There was something different about her. He sensed that she would be around for a long time. And he wasn't exactly certain how he felt about that.

8
BLAZE

It took some prodding, but Nova convinced Blaze to go.

"I think you'll be sorry if you don't," Nova said from the pantry. She entered the kitchen with a jar of her homemade pickles.

"But *you're* not going," Blaze replied, eyeing the picnic basket that sat on the kitchen table bulging with good things to eat.

"Too much walking. And I wasn't really invited anyway," Nova said as she reorganized the contents of the basket. "I think your father would love for this to be just the three of you." Jars, small bags, and plastic containers fit together like the pieces of a puzzle. "This Claire woman must be special. It's odd of him to want you to meet her so early on."

Blaze didn't exactly know what Nova meant by that comment. And Blaze didn't tell Nova that he'd already seen the woman.

Nova tucked some silverware and striped cloth napkins into the basket and nodded approvingly. "There's too much food for just your father and Claire," she said, wiping her hands on her faded gingham apron. "I really want you to go," she added, her eyes doing half the talking.

Blaze fingered through the basket, looking at the food again. He could see pickles, plums, potato chips, deviled eggs, brownies, iced tea, and chicken. "Okay," he said. "For you."

□   □   □

During the drive to the lake it seemed to Blaze that Glenn and Claire were smiling every other minute. The smiles broke across their lips like bubbles, and, more often than not, erupted into laughter. Glenn and Claire already appeared to be comfortable and familiar with each other—which made perfect sense, because Claire worked at the high school with Glenn.

"Claire teaches Art Metals," Glenn had told Blaze that morning. "You know—rings and belt buckles. Things like that." They had been folding an old blanket to use on the picnic. Glenn and Blaze each held two corners, the blanket drooping between them. The piping

46

was coming loose in Blaze's fingers, threads giving way. They drew near to meet, and as Blaze handed his corners to Glenn, he noticed a slightly amused look in his father's eyes.

Glenn also told Blaze how much he admired Claire's artwork. She made jewelry, but her specialty was small ornate boxes of gold and silver, delicately clasped and lined with dark velvet. "Last year was her first year teaching here," Glenn had explained. "And I really want you to meet her, Blazer."

Glenn seldom called his son Blazer—only when he was wildly happy after completing a painting successfully, or on the rare occasion that he had had too much to drink. Neither was the case that morning.

Blaze shifted around in the backseat. He rolled the window up and down. He fussed with the collar of his shirt and pulled it higher around his neck. He fiddled with the handles of the picnic basket. Finally they arrived. Blaze was relieved to be out of the car and into the open air that was busy with a myriad of sounds—birds, insects, and the laughter and voices of other people.

They found a shady spot on the grass to spread the blanket, secluded a bit from the crowd on the beach. The sun sequined the lake and Blaze squinted when he looked at it.

"Isn't it beautiful?" Claire said to no one in particular. She had long legs and arms that she moved gracefully. When she sat down, the skirt she wore over her swimsuit billowed and fell like an umbrella opening and closing.

"You are," Glenn said softly, touching one finger to Claire's sandaled foot. "And you are, too," he said loudly, looking at Blaze. Glenn raised and lowered his eyebrows comically. Then he winked at him.

Blaze could feel himself blush. "Da-a-a-ad," he said.

Throughout lunch Blaze tried to steal glances at Claire. His eyes flitted quickly from one detail to another. Yellow-green eyes. Long streaky blond-gray hair that made him think of animal fur. Skin tanned dark as tea. There was so much to take in, Blaze had to remind himself to chew.

They talked about art and the high school and what a good gardener and cook Nova was. They talked about books and recipes and Blaze's teachers from last year. They talked long after they had finished eating. Claire told Blaze that she had grown up in Chicago and that she liked being in Wisconsin now. Then they talked about art again. Glenn said that he wished he could make enough money painting. He wished that he didn't have to teach. He couldn't think of anything better than the luxury of being able to paint every day without worrying about mortgage payments and bills. And Blaze thought of his own blank canvas.

Although Claire and Glenn tried to include Blaze in the conversation, he tended to nod a lot and give one-word answers and comments. He was busy observing and being shy. He found himself watching Claire's hands.

When they had picked up Claire at her apartment, Blaze had been surprised by the seriousness of her handshake. As Glenn introduced her to Blaze, she held his hand in hers for a long moment as though she really meant it. Her hand had been warm. His had been cold.

After a while they went swimming. Blaze was leery about going in water over his head, so when they did finally go in the deeper water, he rode on Glenn's back while Claire floated beside them. Periodically Claire would swim ahead and then somehow end up surfacing behind them. She'd pop up out of the water, dripping and blinking. Her eyelashes were beaded with water droplets and they sparkled. Her color was high, her movements quick and sure.

"Look at that," Blaze said to Glenn.

Blaze had spotted a wiry towheaded girl and a big bald man not far from where they were. The girl climbed onto the man's shoulders, then jumped off, making an enormous splash. She did it again and again, her laughter growing louder with each jump.

"Want to try it?" Glenn asked.

Blaze tensed, but said, "Yes." His response surprised him. And he even asked Claire to watch.

"We should go a little farther out," Glenn said.

Glenn crouched.

Claire watched.

And Blaze climbed onto Glenn's shoulders, holding on like a clamp. Glenn's birthmark was visible between strands of his hair, between Blaze's thumbs. Blaze hesitated. He took a deep breath, closed his eyes—and jumped.

Blaze's hands were in fists as he hit the water. Then they opened up. And so did his eyes. And so did his mouth. He took a breath under water.

When Blaze surfaced, he was coughing. He grabbed Glenn.

"Are you all right?" Glenn asked, carrying Blaze to shallow water.

Blaze shivered. "Yeah," he said. He coughed some more. "I just swallowed some water."

"That was some jump," said Claire.

Blaze didn't say anything for a moment, and then he told them quietly, "Maybe I'll just sit on the beach for a while." His throat and nose and eyes were burning. He shivered again.

"Want company?" Glenn asked.

Blaze shook his head no. He was embarrassed.

Blaze walked the length of the beach looking at stones. Then he sat at the water's edge, poking his toes at the bubbly fringe that lapped about him, wishing that he knew how to swim.

"Bored?" someone said.

Blaze turned with a start. It was Claire. She wrapped her towel around herself and sat down.

"Where's my dad?" Blaze asked, trying to cross his legs in a manner that would hide the scars on his ankles.

"Over there," Claire said, pointing.

Blaze watched Glenn with a combination of pride and envy. Glenn sliced through the water, his arms cutting perfect angles, his head turning rhythmically.

"He's good," Blaze said. "At swimming. You are, too," he added.

"I didn't know how to swim until I went to college," Claire said. "I could hardly float before that."

"Really?"

Claire nodded and narrowed her lips. "It was one of those things I always wanted to do, and always put off. I still want to learn how to play the piano and speak French." She paused. "Is there anything you really want to learn how to do?"

Blaze was paralyzed by the question. There were so many things he wanted to be able to do. But they would seem so simple to anyone else: Go to sleep without the light on. Go out for the basketball team at school. Pet a big dog without shaking. Ride the Ferris wheel alone.

Sweat dripped down Blaze's face. He touched one corner of his mouth, then the other, with his tongue. "I'd like to fly," he managed to say. "I've never done it."

"In an airplane, or on your own like a bird?" Claire asked, smiling.

Blaze laughed, relieved a bit. "Like a bird," he said, relaxing.

"Me, too," said Claire. She closed her eyes and threw her head back, stretching. She hugged herself. "Wouldn't that be wonderful?"

Two children, holding hands, ran past Blaze and Claire, splashing them.

"You know, that jump you did out there was good," Claire said, her eyes following the children down the sand.

"Really?" Blaze thought it had been terribly clumsy, not to mention all his coughing.

"Good jump," Claire said. She ran her fingers through her hair. "Good jump," she repeated, her face slanted upward as though she were talking to the sun.

They stayed on the beach, side by side, silently. Without realizing it, Blaze had untucked his legs and begun rubbing his ankles. The blister-smooth skin was vivid in the sun, the rippled areas emphasized like tiny raised cursive writing. Suddenly, Blaze noticed that Claire had been watching him; he saw her looking at his ankles. When their eyes met, Claire didn't turn away; she just smiled naturally.

And then, for some reason, Blaze told her about the fire.

How he had been waiting in line to ride the Ferris

wheel on the Fourth of July after Reena died. How there had been a short circuit. How the electrical wires that lay at his feet sizzled and jumped like snakes on fire. He told her about the awful smell in the ambulance. Even about the paramedic who tried to comfort him by telling him that both his father and mother could ride with him to the hospital. And how—during a confusing minute—he asked for Reena, even though she was dead.

When Blaze finished he felt numb and weightless. He thought he might rise off the beach and drift above the lake like fog, the way he did in his father's paintings.

9
BLAZE

"Well, what do you think?" Glenn asked. They were driving home after dropping Claire off at her apartment.

Blaze shrugged. "I don't know," he said. "What do *you* think?"

"I like her," Glenn answered, lightly tapping out a rhythm on the steering wheel. "I like her a lot." Glenn looked sideways at Blaze. "Is that okay with you? I'd like it to be."

"I guess," Blaze replied. "She's pretty."

"She is, isn't she?" Glenn said, smiling. "And smart and artistic and nice . . ."

"Are you going to marry her?"

Glenn let out a quick laugh. "Not tonight," he said, joking.

"No, really, are you going to?"

Glenn lowered his voice. "It's too early to tell. But I know that we have a lot in common. We have a good time when we're together, too." He paused. "I've known Claire for a year at school now . . ." His voice trailed off. And he smiled a big smile again.

Blaze thought it was a goofy smile, like the smiles he drew with crayons when he was three. It made Blaze feel good to see Glenn so happy. And at the same time it was scary. What if Glenn *did* marry Claire Becker? What would their life be like? How would it change?

Blaze watched the passing clouds, searching for different shapes in them: a car; a cow; a wizened, bearded man. It had only been hours since he had told Claire about the fire, and already he regretted it. Why had he revealed so much to a near stranger? Claire was pretty; was that why? At least he hadn't told her everything. He hadn't told her about the skin grafting or how hard he had cried. And he hadn't told her *why* he had been waiting in line for the Ferris wheel.

"Do you mind if we stop at the grocery store?" Glenn asked. "I should pick up a few things."

"Okay," said Blaze.

Glenn hummed in the parking lot. He raced Blaze up and down the aisles. And, laughing musically, he plucked oranges from a display and tossed them to Blaze directly in front of a sullen-faced man who shook his head and clucked his tongue disapprovingly.

After grocery shopping they stopped for ice cream.

Sitting on the curb in the muggy afternoon air, spumoni dripping down his wrist, Blaze wished that he could see the future. He wished that he could see ahead to the end of summer, to Christmas, to the following summer. He wished that he could know for sure what would be happening to his family. He wished he knew what was happening now.

□　　□　　□

Blaze's mind was muzzy. He was thinking about his mother. He rolled over on his stomach and his bed squeaked. Sometimes he would forget exactly what his mother looked like, and he would have to study a photograph. Sometimes what he could remember was clouded. Sometimes he and Glenn would look at old photographs and mementos together, and it would make Blaze feel calm and edgy at the same time.

After a few minutes, Blaze flipped over on his back again. He thought of the fire and the Ferris wheel and Claire and what he *hadn't* told her. . . .

Reena rode the Ferris wheel with Blaze shortly before she died. It was the last thing they did together before Reena went to the hospital for the final time. They were at the fairgrounds on the Fourth of July. Glenn watched and waited while they rode. It was a small Ferris wheel, part of a small fair that came to town every July. There were rides and game booths and bright billowy tents where food was sold. Two weather-beaten wooden sol-

diers marked the entrance. They looked like the un-
wanted toys of a giant, dropped into the trees and
forgotten.

The next year he wanted to do it by himself. For her.
It was something he had to do. It was very important to
him. He begged Glenn to let him try it. It was a small
Ferris wheel, made for children, so Glenn said yes,
bought him a ticket, and watched and waited again.

But Blaze needed the help of a friend. So he made
one up. Benny was his name. Blaze whispered to Benny
while he moved closer and closer to the man taking tick-
ets. That was the year of the fire. Of course, he didn't
go through with it *that* year. So he buried Benny. And
then came Ajax.

Good-bye, Benny.

The following year Blaze had to ask to go to the fairgrounds. "Are you sure you want to go?" Glenn asked.
Blaze was sure. "We can just walk around," said Glenn.

Blaze hadn't heard Glenn and Nova talk about insur-
ance money and doctor bills for a long time. And Glenn
told Blaze that a different company was running the fair
now. The big wooden soldiers were gone, but there was
still a Ferris wheel. It looked enough like the one he had
ridden with Reena to count. It was small, with wire cages
that spun gently as the wheel rotated.

"I want to try it," Blaze said.

"Okay," said Glenn. "Let's do it."

"I want to try it alone," said Blaze.

Glenn let him try.

But it was more difficult than he thought it would be. He worried about the Ferris wheel itself. He remembered the cords that had caught on fire. He thought about his mother. He couldn't do it. Ajax didn't help. "I changed my mind," he told Glenn. "Can we get something to eat?"

Good-bye, Ajax.

He tries every year. He doesn't want to be afraid.

Good-bye, Ken.

He stands in line, but turns away at the last minute. He goes on other rides.

Good-bye, Harold.

Now that he's old enough to go to the fairgrounds with some of his classmates, he sneaks off alone to the Ferris wheel. Unsuccessful every time. Or if his classmates want to ride the Ferris wheel, he says, "I have to go to the bathroom—do it without me." Or "I'm going back to the games for a while. Meet me there."

Good-bye, Ortman.

Every year that he can't ride the Ferris wheel, he buries his old friend and gets a new one.

Every year he tells no one.

Every year he digs another hole.

BLAZE

Blaze had a dream that didn't frighten him, but time and place and all other particulars escaped him. He stared listlessly at a spot on the ceiling in his bedroom, trying to make the dream come back. But he could only remember a foggy, pleasant feeling, and he tried to hold on to it, grabbing his chest as if the feeling were touchable and could be hugged like a pillow.

After looking out the window and checking the hill (no new words of stone), Blaze dressed and went down to the kitchen for breakfast. Nova made pancakes for him. She served them with butter, blueberries, and powdered sugar. Blaze played with the blueberries, forming a letter *C* with them on the top of his stack of pancakes.

"Do you like her?" Nova asked.

"Who?" Blaze said. He spread some of the blueberries to the edge of his plate.

"Claire, of course," Nova replied. "Who else would I mean?" She smiled at Blaze and her cheeks became a farmer's field of wrinkles.

"I'm not sure," Blaze answered, raising his fork, a blueberry speared on each tine. "But I think Dad's in love." The word sounded funny to Blaze: *love*. He wrinkled his nose.

"Love's not such a bad thing."

"I know, I know," Blaze said, tossing his head from side to side. He smiled at Nova. "You really wouldn't care if he got married again?"

"I'd love it, and I mean it, and you know it. We've talked about that before."

"Would you still live with us?"

Nova shook her head yes. "But don't you think you're jumping the gun? Slow down a bit. Eat your breakfast."

He ate and he thought. He thought that Nova was the most calm person he knew. And the smartest. And the nicest. He thought about going to rummage sales that afternoon with Glenn and Claire; Claire was looking for old furniture to fix up for her apartment. He thought about being short and wondered how tall he would be when he was fully grown. And he thought that he wanted to eat another pancake. And he did.

After finishing breakfast and helping Nova with the

dishes, Blaze walked up the hill to the black locust tree. He seemed drawn there as if by a magnet. It would be a hot day. Earlier there had been a milky haze on the hill that burned off, but the air was still heavy. Dew glittered on the tips of the grass. As he approached the crest of the hill, Blaze swung his arms back and forth, pretending to cut through the heat. When he reached the top, he stopped suddenly.

Within the border of the grave site were more messages. This time the words were formed with small stones and pebbles, each letter only a few inches tall at most. The stones spelled YOU'RE ON FIRE and FIRE! The words were written in an arc near the trunk of the black locust tree. The exclamation point that ended it was long and wiggly like a worm.

□   □   □

"Come on," Glenn coaxed, slapping the upholstery beside him. "We're running late."

"I'm not going with you," Blaze said slowly, his eyes narrow because of the sun.

"What's up?" Glenn asked. He had been waiting in the car for Blaze, the motor idling. He was ready to pick up Claire and had been signaling Blaze by honking the horn.

Blaze shrugged. He didn't feel like talking. He knew the words would catch in his throat, possibly making him cry. He also knew that he never wanted to see Claire

Becker again. Now there was no doubt in his mind who was responsible for the words of stone. Claire Becker. A swift internal pull convinced him this was the truth. He had told Claire about the fire, and she had used the information for a cruel joke.

Glenn turned off the ignition. "Are you okay?"

"I think I ate too much for breakfast," Blaze said, holding his stomach. "It's not a big deal, but I think I should stay home."

"Would you rather I stayed home, too? I can call Claire."

"No," Blaze said. "You should go."

"Okay," Glenn said, almost like a question. "I hope you feel better." He started the car again. "See you later," he called.

Blaze waved. He had figured out who had written the words of stone. But what would he do now?

JOSELLE

Joselle was examining a scab on her knee when the phone rang. She jumped up to get it, but since the only phone in the house sat on the end table beside the rocking chair where Floy happened to be planted, her chances of answering it were next to none. After a pleasant hello, Floy's voice took on an icy edge. Joselle knew instantly that The Beautiful Vicki was on the line. Floy's face seemed to deflate and her lips pursed. Nearly everything about her became tight, and yet she cradled the phone against her shoulder and continued to work on her needlepoint. Her fingers moved like dancers, pushing and pulling, bringing a garden to life with thread. Lilacs, tulips, and daffodils bloomed between her hands.

Her silver needle glinted and Joselle thought of sparks. Even when Floy sighed heavily or rolled her eyes, her fingers continued to flow at the same rhythmic pace.

Joselle picked her scab while she listened. Then she drew her knee up to her mouth and bit off the scab. She swallowed hard and licked her wound.

"How can you afford that?" Floy asked. "What about your job at the restaurant?"

Joselle could feel her heartbeat quicken. She began playing "The Star-Spangled Banner" loudly on her teeth.

"Don't worry about Joselle," Floy said. "Good *heavens,* of course you should talk to her. Just a minute."

Floy handed the receiver to Joselle.

"Joselle?" Vicki said.

"Hi," Joselle answered reluctantly, flexing her toes inside her shoes.

"Sorry I didn't send you a postcard or call sooner. . . ." There was an awkward pause. "Uh, Rick and I decided we'd like to see the ocean—the Pacific Ocean. So we're going to be gone longer than we thought. It's a far way from Wisconsin, you know. But anyway, your grandmother's glad to have you there. And—don't worry—I checked it out with the restaurant. They'll give me my job back when I get home."

"Why can't I come with you?"

"Come on, Joselle. We're already on the road. And Rick doesn't want this to be a kid's vacation. We need a break. *I* need a break from *you*. You know how we get when we're together too long. This is good for you, too."

Joselle didn't want to pay attention any more. She tried to twirl the phone like a baton, but dropped it on the floor. She picked it up, hesitated a moment, then spoke into the receiver very clearly. "I might have blood poisoning," she said, curling her lip. "But if anything happens I'm sure someone will be able to locate you." Without waiting for a response, she gently hung up the phone.

Joselle and Floy looked at each other.

"I don't want to talk about it," Joselle said, turning her eyes away.

"Me neither," said Floy, placing her needlepoint on the end table and standing. She grabbed her sweater from the back of the chair and draped it over her shoulders. "The mall's open late tonight. Let's go shopping."

□   □   □

The air in the mall smelled stale—of popcorn, smoke, sweat, and perfume—but it was a hopeful smell; it carried with it the prospect of new things to take home. When Joselle shopped at malls with Vicki, they rarely bought anything. They purchased most of their clothes at resale shops. Vicki tried to convince Joselle that the clothes from Retro Fashions and Goldie's Oldies were more chic anyway, but Joselle knew that Vicki couldn't afford shopping at the other stores. And yet they went to them on a regular basis "just to look." Joselle disliked the whole routine because she often saw things that she wanted badly, knowing full well that she couldn't have them. She'd pout all the way home, bewildered by the injustice of it all. She referred to this practice as "visiting clothes." Last year for Mrs. Weynand's language arts class, Joselle wrote an essay about "visiting" a pair of tight, stone-washed jeans so many times that she became best friends with them. Mrs. Weynand said the essay showed a great deal of creativity but was lacking in other areas—namely grammar, spelling, and punctuation. She gave it a C-minus.

Joselle felt only slightly guilty that Floy was spending so much money on her. But Floy was the one pushing certain items, as though an extra pair of tights or some dangly rhinestone earrings could fill Joselle up until there was no room for unhappiness. When Joselle expressed an interest in a fuchsia tank top, Floy insisted that she have the black-and-white striped one, too. And Floy wouldn't take no for an answer when she saw the way Joselle's eyes widened as she stroked a peach cashmere sweater that had buttons like pearls.

"You'd look beautiful in that," Floy said, scooping it up and holding it in front of Joselle.

"Grammy, I was just looking," Joselle said, turning away. She had seen the price tag. She knew how expensive it was.

"It's got your name written all over it," Floy said. "Just think how envious your classmates will be next school year."

Joselle considered this and felt herself weakening. Even Sherry Gerke, who often made a point of criticizing Joselle's wardrobe in front of anyone who would listen in the girls' rest room, would have nothing but good things to say about *this* sweater. It was classy. Joselle cackled to herself.

"Okay, Grammy, you win," Joselle said, throwing up her hands. "I'll take it."

As they marched up to the checkout counter together, Joselle had to concentrate hard to keep her fingers from crawling onto Floy's arm and tugging the sweater away from her.

"Forget the bag," Joselle told the clerk. "I'm wearing it!"

Floy nodded approval.

"Thanks, Grammy!" Joselle shrieked. "Now you're sure this is okay?" she added in a very serious voice.

"Yes," Floy answered. "A good splurge every now and then does wonders."

But Joselle repeated the question over and over because she had noticed the way the corner of Floy's mouth had twitched upward, forming a thick indented comma deep in her cheek as she wrote out the check to pay for the sweater.

"If you ask me one more time, I'll start calling you a

broken record," Floy finally said, swatting Joselle softly on her behind. "Come on, we need to find some nail polish before the stores close."

On the drive home, the stars were brighter than Joselle had ever seen. And the evening smelled of grapes. Fireflies dotted either side of the highway as if there had been too many stars for the sky to hold and some had spilled downward. Joselle rubbed the buttons on her new sweater, pretending that they were tiny stars that had lost their light. And then, because she wanted the way she felt at that precise moment to last forever, she stuck her head out the window and gulped the air that rushed at her face, hoping that it would work some kind of magic inside her. Hoping that it would make her life perfect in every way.

12

JOSELLE

Joselle woke up with a headache, and there was a pinching sensation behind her eyes. She blinked her eyes quickly and steadily, hoping the feeling would stop, but all it did was intensify the dull pain and make her see double for a minute. Gary heard her stir and raised his head. He slept on the floor alongside the sofa every night now. Right by Joselle. He nudged her hand with his nose until she petted him. Simultaneously, he wagged his tail and yawned twice, like an echo. Joselle covered her face with her arm. "I feel bad, but you smell worse," she told him.

Despite the heat, she had slept in her new sweater. It had transformed her ratty cotton nightgown into the elegant party dress of a princess. Joselle slid off the sofa and pirouetted to the kitchen, trying to work off the way she felt. Gary snapped playfully at the frayed edge of her nightgown as though her dance were a game created especially for him.

Now, on top of having a headache, Joselle became dizzy. After sitting at the table and counting to one hundred, she thought that food might help. She made a three-minute egg, a piece of toast, and a cup of tea with four spoonfuls of sugar and enough milk to turn the tea pale and lukewarm.

After breakfast, Joselle felt better. Floy was still asleep, so Joselle tried extra hard to be quiet. Joselle wondered if Floy couldn't pull herself out of bed because she regretted spending so much money on Joselle. Joselle pictured her grandmother flat in bed, lethargic as a wet wool blanket, exhausted by the shopping spree and clutching an overdrawn check book. The thought nagged at her, and it just got worse when she retrieved all her purchases from the closet and spread them out on the sofa. There were two pairs of tights, two tank tops, a bikini, earrings, socks, four bottles of nail polish, and, of course, the sweater. Joselle knew that if The Beautiful Vicki hadn't phoned about her prolonged trip the sofa would be empty. Floy would never have permitted Joselle to buy the bikini or the dangly earrings. They would have been completely forbidden if Floy hadn't felt sorry for Joselle. Maybe she thinks she's partially responsible, Joselle said to herself. After all, Vicki's her daughter.

Joselle had a fashion show. She tried on each new item and paraded around in front of Gary. He cocked his head, his ears alert, his tail sweeping the floor. But somehow the effect had worn off for Joselle. Last night, in the dressing rooms at the mall, she had been electric with anticipation. She had sniffed everything she tried on, intoxicated by the scent of newness. And on the ride home, buried beneath the shopping bags, her happiness had been a dazzling white spot. Now, sitting on the floor, picking Gary's wheat-colored hair off her rainbow-print bikini, Joselle was a brightly swirled, empty lump of self-pity. She could have gulped enough air last night to fill a hot-air balloon and it wouldn't have mattered. No magic had been worked. Her life would probably never be perfect.

With only her bikini on, Joselle's ball-point-pen tattoos were visible on her thigh. They had worn off a bit, so she took out her pen and wrote over them again, carefully tracing each letter. REENA. FIRE! YOU'RE ON FIRE. And then she added a new one: ORPHAN. And she wasn't entirely certain if she was referring to Blaze Werla or to herself.

□   □   □

The distance between Joselle's house and the Pacific Ocean seemed endless. After the fashion show, Joselle discovered a road atlas on Floy's bookshelf, and her finger followed the red and blue lines that indicated highways, weaving across the country until they ended at

Route 101 on the coast. The number of miles that sepa-
rated Wisconsin and the ocean was so staggering, her
finger quivered. On the map, the crisscrossed network
of roads looked like a maze—much too disorienting for
Vicki to negotiate. Joselle hoped that Rick was doing
most of the driving.

At least Rick was a good driver. In Joselle's opinion,
Rick's only other talent was turning his eyelids inside
out. It was one of the most disgusting things Joselle had
ever seen, but he was very good at it. Another disgusting
thing about Rick was his hair. The hair on the top of his
head was okay—short, brown, straight, thick. But the
hair on the rest of him wasn't okay. It sprouted from the
backs of his hands and from under his shirt collars like
twisty forests. The sight of it made Joselle want to throw
up. Rick was rangy and languid. He hunched his shoulders frequently, and a perfect pimple flourished on the
bridge of his nose. Vicki said that Rick was good at his
job; he was an electrician. But Joselle thought that he
was too absentminded and too interested in ESP to be
working with things as dangerous as power sources and
currents. She hoped that he would never rewire their
house.

Sadly, Joselle envisioned Rick and Vicki lost and
confused in Nebraska or stranded on some dirt road
in Wyoming. And yet, ironically, part of her wished
that the car *would* overheat, that they *would* run out
of gas, and that they *would* get flat tires. A minute

later, she wished them a speedy, safe trip, and she longed for Vicki so intensely that her eyes turned misty.

Joselle had never been out of southern Wisconsin, and she realized how small an area this was compared to the rest of the country, not to mention the world. She and Vicki lived in a small brick ranch house in Kenosha. Floy lived in the country outside of Madison. They were only a few hours apart by car, and yet they only saw each other two or three times a year. And it was nearly always Floy who did the visiting. If I ever make it out of the Midwest I'll probably faint, Joselle thought. Her father, who she had only seen once, supposedly lived in Texas. She never heard from him, and Vicki cringed whenever his name was mentioned, so Joselle didn't bother thinking about him very often. And she never asked Vicki to talk about him—that was hitting below the belt and she knew it. She could be awful, but not that awful. Joselle owned one photograph of him that she kept in the bottom of her sock drawer. The photograph was dog-eared and slightly out of focus, but Joselle could make out a man who she thought looked devastatingly handsome or evil as a snake, depending on her mood. His name was Jerry Hefko, and in the photo he was posing on a motorcycle wearing sunglasses and a red bandanna on his head. Dense black curls hung to his shoulders. Although neither Joselle nor Vicki had ever used Hefko as a last name, Joselle had secretly carved JOSELLE HEFKO on one leg of the kitchen table with a paring knife when she was seven and furious at her mother for something or other.

"Why do people live in certain places?" she asked Gary, staring at Texas.

Gary tipped his head and knitted his brow.

"I mean, why wasn't I born in New York or Miami? Someplace glamorous?"

"Planning a trip?" Floy asked in a voice thick and raspy with morning, startling Joselle. She shuffled across the floor in her fuzzy slippers.

"Nope," Joselle said, closing the atlas and replacing it on the shelf. "I was just killing time waiting for you to get up. Sleepyhead."

Between stretches and yawns, Floy banged around the kitchen making coffee.

"I checked on you five times, you know," Joselle said. "I wanted to make sure you were breathing."

Floy flicked her wrist and glanced at her watch. "It's only seven-fifteen. This is when I always get up. How long have you been awake?"

And only then did Joselle realize how early she had gotten up. She figured it had been hours since she awoke. "I don't know," is all she said.

Floy sipped her coffee, savoring every drop, as though it eased some discomfort. Her cup sounded like a tiny bell when it clinked against the saucer. "I thought I'd cut the grass today. If you're not too busy, I could use some help."

Joselle's chin crumpled. She hated yard work. "Well, actually," she said, "considering everything that's been happening to me lately I think I might need time alone today to contemplate my future."

Floy only nodded and looked away, her deep-set gray eyes focusing on the coffeepot.

"I'm probably helping you by *not* helping you," Joselle offered, her voice confident and round. "I'm usually much more trouble than I'm worth."

□   □   □

The lawn mower roared in Joselle's ears, but she walked right past Floy and toward the hill undaunted. Sometimes she hated herself for the way she treated people, for her selfishness. And yet, she seemed to have no control over her behavior. It's not my fault I am the way I am, she thought.

The sky was the blue of a baby's blanket and the clouds looked like massive heads of cauliflower. Joselle slapped her thigh and whispered, "Orphan." She couldn't decide if she should write the new word with stones as she had done with the other words or try something different. She wondered how Blaze Werla had been reacting to her messages. She hoped he was going crazy with confusion. Maybe this time I should write the word and then hide behind a bush and wait till he appears, she thought. Maybe I could see him cry.

But as it turned out, Joselle's plan was not workable. She skipped to the top of the hill and stopped suddenly, frozen. Blaze Werla was crouching beside the big tree. And before Joselle could move, their eyes met. And locked together.

BLAZE

The first time Blaze saw her, the hair on the back of his neck prickled. Although the sun was shining, he swore that she had no shadow, and despite the fact that she stood perfectly still and there was no wind, her dangly rhinestone earrings jiggled, making thin music. Her eyes appeared to be entirely black—like hard, shiny pieces of licorice. They were so hypnotic, Blaze had to work at forcing his eyes to break contact with hers. When she came closer he noticed that she smelled dusty, like a ladybug. And then she smiled. Her smile did anything but put him at ease. Her smile was enormous and glassy and sharp.

"Big teeth," was all he managed to say, walking backward as if in a trance.

The girl thrust out her hand, her fingers grazing Blaze's chest. "I'm Joselle Stark," she announced grandly.

Blaze's fingers felt dwarfed and breakable in hers. She had the grip of a man.

"The old lady that lives over there is my grandmother," Joselle said, pointing toward Floy Stark's neat, square house. "I'm staying with her for a bit while my mother explores the Pacific Ocean. She's kind of a scientist—my mother. My grandmother's just a grandmother." While she spoke she tossed her head and flared her nostrils. "So," she said, "who are you?"

Blaze could barely speak. His words cracked and melted. "My name is Blaze," he finally offered in a scratchy whisper.

"That's an odd name."

Blaze shrugged and scuffed his shoes.

"You're so *little*, too," Joselle said in a thrilled voice, rumpling his hair. "And if it wasn't impossible, I'd swear you were shrinking right before my very eyes."

Looking down, Blaze scanned his entire body, checking to make sure that he wasn't, in fact, becoming smaller. And then, as though he had no control over what he was saying, words spilled out of his mouth like the beads of a breaking necklace: "I'm the smallest in my class. I am every year."

"No kidding," Joselle said sarcastically. "It wouldn't take a brain to figure that out. Unless you go to school with midgets."

Blaze only fidgeted, regretful.

"Well, who cares anyway?" Joselle said, marching in place. Then she strutted around the black locust tree like a queen. "All I can say is—just look at this view! I've never been up here before. It's tremendously fantastic." She cleared her throat. "I just arrived today, you know," she said, turning her head toward Blaze, her eyes thin as slits. Because she wasn't looking ahead, Joselle tripped over one of Blaze's stones. Dust rose, veiling her as she stumbled and fell. Her knees and hands were streaked with dirt.

"Are you okay?" Blaze asked shyly, lightly nudging the stone with his shoe.

"I'll live," Joselle answered, her face bunched. And then suddenly her mood swung and she smiled again. This time gleefully. "Hey, look, I'm injured," she said merrily, pushing her knee at Blaze. Marking the middle of her knee was a perfect drop of blood. "It's an enchanted liquid ruby," Joselle whispered. "I'll seize it like this," she said, wiping her knee with her finger. "I'll share it with you like this," she continued, smearing blood on Blaze's leg. "And then I'll seal the magic like this," she told him, licking her finger several times. "Now we're true friends. Forever."

Blaze pulled the edge of his T-shirt into his mouth and bit down, and because he was breathing so hard, his mouth sounded like the wind. "I'd better go," he said tentatively, moving away. In his mind, he was already home, lying on his bed with the door closed.

"Come back tomorrow," Joselle called. "You have to. Same time. Same place."

Blaze ran all the way down the hill. As he tore through the weeds and grass, his arms making huge loops in the air, he felt as though he were emerging from a terrible and wonderful spell.

□   □   □

Thoughts of the girl stayed with Blaze all afternoon like a film on his skin. She baffled him and intrigued him. His mind strayed to her even as he set the table for dinner. He saw her face in each plate and bowl. Her teeth and her eyes materialized vaguely on the china like the Cheshire cat.

The day had grown hotter and hotter, so they were going to have a big salad and gazpacho. "Too hot to use the oven today," Nova repeated as she moved around the kitchen. Her skin had taken on a sweaty sheen. When she turned from reaching for the large wooden salad bowl in the cupboard, her forehead glistened and Blaze noticed damp saggy half-moons under her arms on her thin housedress. The heat didn't bother him nearly as much as it did Nova.

Glenn was slicing hard-boiled eggs for the salad. It had been just over a week ago that he had introduced Claire to Blaze and Nova. Since then, he had been spending a considerable amount of time doing domestic things: helping to make dinner, washing dishes, shopping for groceries. He wasn't painting nearly as intensely as he usually did.

"I'm going to freshen up before Claire arrives," Nova said. She flapped her dress and sighed. "Too hot," she murmured on her way upstairs to change clothes.

"You seem quiet," Glenn said to Blaze.

"Not really."

"Well, then talk to me," Glenn said as he arranged the eggs on a ruffly bed of various lettuces from Nova's garden. "How are you?"

"I dunno," Blaze answered, and it was purely the truth. He didn't know. And if *he* didn't know, how could he give his feelings a name and discuss them? He had too much to think about. Claire. And now Joselle Stark.

"I understand how you might feel about Claire," Glenn said. "I do . . ." He smiled his assurance and squeezed the back of Blaze's neck.

"I know," Blaze replied, hoping that he sounded cheerful and cooperative. But Glenn couldn't understand. Blaze hadn't told him about the words of stone.

At first it had made perfect sense that Claire had been the one to write them. Blaze had told her about the fire, and the next morning the words appeared. But since then Claire had acted completely normal—whatever that meant for someone you hardly knew.

Although Blaze had tried to avoid Claire, she still treated him kindly, which puzzled him. Even if he had been ignoring her throughout an entire meal, she would present small gestures—a look, a grin, a compliment—that would cause Blaze to drop his silverware.

□   □   □

"I have something for you, Blaze," Claire said when she arrived. "Come to my car."

It occurred to Blaze that he could pretend not to have heard her. He could just walk past her into the kitchen to get something to nibble on while he waited for dinner. He followed her to her car.

"Your dad told me that he had given you a canvas to work on. I thought you might like to have your own paints." Claire opened the car door and pulled out a box the size of a portable TV. She placed the box on the ground and opened it up so Blaze could see inside. "I know you have watercolors, but these are acrylics. They're my old ones—I don't use them anymore."

There must have been thirty tubes of paint. Blaze could tell that some of the tubes had been used, but others looked brand new.

"I know your dad would let you use his oil paints in his studio, but this way you can paint in your own room if you like. Whenever you want. And you can clean up with water. They're easy."

"Thank you," said Blaze. He turned the tubes in his hand, reading the names of the colors.

"The brushes are in here," Claire told him, picking up

a long, thin manila envelope that was tucked in the side of the box. She took out one of the brushes and pretended to paint in the air. Her wrist moved gracefully, round and round. "Well, I'm going to see if Nova needs any help in the kitchen," Claire said, handing the brush to Blaze.

"Thank you," Blaze said again.

"You're welcome."

Blaze carried the box to the porch and sat down. The tubes of paint reminded him of party favors frozen in various stages. The kind that unroll as you blow into them, then collapse on themselves as the air escapes, curling up. Blaze was familiar with most of the colors because of Glenn: cadmium red, alizarine crimson, burnt umber, cobalt blue, yellow ocher. He pretended to paint in the air as Claire had done. He was beginning to get excited about starting his canvas.

His certainty that Claire was responsible for the words of stone had been a knot lodged inside his chest. The knot was gradually loosening. Blaze was glad that he had waited, that he hadn't said anything to Glenn.

"*Was* it my imagination, Simon?" Blaze asked. He wanted to convince himself of that. He told himself it wouldn't be surprising, given that it was July. His dreams were proof of the power of his imagination.

He would wait. He would push it out of his mind. After all, he had something new to concern himself with: Joselle Stark. She had said they were true friends—and yet they barely knew each other. If they *did* become true friends, maybe he could tell her about the words of stone. Maybe she'd know what to do.

A spider hanging motionless in its web caught his eye. The web was a perfect, intricate hexagon strung between two posts of the porch railing. Blaze didn't like spiders particularly, except from a distance. He pictured Joselle Stark approaching this spider easily and touching it with her finger. Blaze knew he would go to the hill tomorrow. He wondered if she would be there.

14
BLAZE

"**F**or the first couple years of your life, you were probably no bigger than a salt shaker," Joselle told Blaze, cupping her hand and holding it out to indicate size. "In fact, it's probably a miracle you lived. I'll bet your parents have photographs from when you were three, but they tell you they were from the day you were born." Joselle brushed a tangle of hair away from her eyes. "Parents do things like that," she added crisply, snapping her fingers.

Blaze wondered exactly what Joselle meant. She confused him completely, but at the same time she spoke with such authority that he was compelled to accept as true everything she said. "I was little, but not *that* little," he mumbled at last, blushing a bit, opening and closing his fists.

"Believe what you have to," Joselle said, shaking her head.

It was only their second time together. They were sitting beneath the black locust tree, within the semicircle of Blaze's stones. He hoped that Joselle wouldn't ask about the stones, or worse, move them. Whenever Joselle poked at them with her foot or gazed at them for what seemed like a long time, Blaze felt a small tremor in his leg. He could never explain his stones to this curious girl who reminded him of wild, impish, confident children he had only known in books.

"Want some?" Joselle asked, lifting the necklace of popcorn she was wearing over her head and offering it to Blaze. "Popcorn. Fresh popcorn," she called, making her voice sound important.

"Thanks," said Blaze, pulling off a few kernels. Bewitched, he handed the necklace back. Each time he chewed and swallowed, his teeth creaked and his throat tickled.

"I always get the hulls stuck on my teeth. And always my tooth with the micro-dot," Joselle said.

"What's that?"

"It's this teensy-weensy thing printed on my tooth with my name, address, and birthday. You can't even see it with the naked eye. I used to think it was really neat until I realized it would only do any good if they found me dead. You know, to identify me."

Blaze tried to absorb this, but his mind kept stumbling

on the word dead. It made him shiver. And of course, he thought of his mother. He could see an image of her, memorized from a photograph, so clearly among the leaves above him that he thought he could make the image stay there forever. But the breeze fluttered, the leaves stirred, and she disappeared. "My mother is dead," he heard himself say.

For once, the girl seemed to be at a loss for words. Wrapped in absolute silence, Blaze watched her. Joselle twisted her popcorn necklace, then pushed and pulled pieces of popcorn as though she were moving counters on an abacus. She appeared to be so deep in thought that Blaze wondered if he could see what she was thinking in the air around her if he looked hard enough.

"Well, you're not the only one," she suddenly blurted out, one large tear sliding down her face. "My father is dead." She placed her necklace over Blaze's head, draping it crookedly across his shoulders. "Welcome to the orphans' club," she sniffed. "The saddest club of all." Then she kissed his cheek sharply and quickly before vanishing behind the slope of the hill.

15
BLAZE

"That's about all I know," said Nova. "But if you like her, it would be nice to have someone to play with. Someone so close." She moved her basket up a few feet and continued picking beans. The plants were heavy with pods that ranged in color from milky yellow to emerald. The sizes and shapes varied, too. Some beans were huge and so swollen they looked surreal. Others were narrow and small and straight as nails. "Is she here for a long visit, or a short one?"

"She didn't say exactly," Blaze answered. He was sitting in the row next to Nova eating a bean. Mist tickled his eyes when he snapped it. "Her father died," he said.

"I wasn't aware of that," Nova said. She really didn't

know much about Joselle Stark. Or her mother. "I'm not even too familiar with Floy," Nova told him. "We greet one another, but that's about it. I guess the hill is big enough and our houses are far enough apart to keep our lives separate." Nova took off her hat and fanned herself with it. "Would you like to have Joselle over for lunch?" she asked. "Egg salad sandwiches? With home-grown beans and homegrown lettuce?"

"Not today. But maybe sometime." Would Joselle say yes if he asked her? Possibly. After all, she had kissed him. Blaze had never been kissed by a girl before. Just thinking about it made his heart anxious. And he thought about it a lot. No one had ever been so interest-ing to him before. And to have Joselle confide in him about her father bonded them.

When Nova finished picking her row, she pointed to the tomato plants. "I've got more tomato plants this year than ever. If they all ripen, we'll have enough tomato sauce and chili relish and salsa for the entire town," she said. She heaved her basket of beans into her arms and sighed. "I'm going inside to start blanching these. And I'm hoping that my legs don't fall off first. Bad circula-tion," she added matter-of-factly.

Blaze watched Nova trudge through the garden and across the lawn. Her thick, corded veins seemed to pulse with each step. Blaze wandered over to his favorite cor-ner of the garden, glancing over his shoulder at Nova until the back door shut behind her. In the corner, a stand of sunflowers formed a wall. Slivers of blue, blue sky shone through the lattice of leaves and huge drooping yellow flowers. When the wind hastened, Blaze could smell the basil, which was planted in a raised bed near the sunflowers. Sometimes he'd pick some of the basil leaves and rub them on a small patch of his arm near his wrist, tinting it green. Then, periodically throughout the day, he'd bring his arm up to his face and inhale deeply. Last year, he had hung a big bunch of basil from the doorknob in his room; the room smelled wonderful for nearly a week. It was amazing to Blaze that everything that was so alive and leafy and aromatic and productive in Nova's garden had begun as tiny seeds. The whole process was one of the most hopeful things he knew. Thinking about Joselle Stark was hopeful, too. Blaze wondered how long she would be staying with her grandmother. He hoped she'd at least stay until school started in the fall.

Blaze wanted to do something special for Joselle because he felt so badly about her father. He wanted to give her some kind of gift. He lay down under the sunflowers, trying to think of something appropriate. It wasn't long before he fell asleep, dreaming, as the morning crept away slowly without him.

□   □   □

The only things of value that Blaze had to offer Joselle were his lost key collection and his Noah's ark. He didn't think he could bear to part with the ark—and besides, he could picture Joselle commenting on how infantile it was—so he gladly put that thought out of his mind. The key collection would also be hard to give up, but not having it around would be something he would just have to get used to. At any rate, the lost key collection wasn't serving its purpose. Blaze had collected the keys and kept them near his bed while he slept with the secret hope that they might open the locked doors that often appeared in his dreams. Usually Reena's voice came from behind the doors, calling him. It was a stupid idea anyway, Blaze thought. A real key can't open something in a dream.

He looked at each key carefully, trying to remember where it had been found or who had given it to him. When he placed the mason jar that held the keys in a box and sealed it, he had a premonition that he would wake up in the middle of the night, panicked and needing the keys. "I hope I'm doing the right thing, Simon," he whispered. Regretfully, he wrapped the box in the comics from the previous Sunday's newspaper, tied a limp bow on top with red yarn, and held it tightly on his lap until he knew he was ready to meet Joselle on the hill.

□   □   □

As she opened the box, Blaze detected first amusement, then baffled uncertainty in Joselle's look. After a moment she shrieked lustily and said, "Oh, I get it—you think you have the key to my heart." She batted her eyelids and preened herself, obviously enjoying her remark.

"It's not a joke. It's a present."

"Oh, piffle, piddle," she said airily. "Don't be so serious all the time."

Blaze tried to explain his feelings about Joselle's father, but only got frustrated.

"Let's play a game," said Joselle, barely allowing Blaze a word. "It's called Personal Scent. It'll just take me a minute to get ready."

Blaze watched Joselle. She unrolled the top of a brown paper sack from the local grocery store and opened it up. The bag was soft and crumpled from use, from being held by sweaty hands. One by one, Joselle took out small glass bottles of various sizes filled with different colored liquids. She lined them up between them like a tiny fence.

"Like I said, the game is called Personal Scent. And I, Joselle Stark, am Keeper of the Scents." She shook the mason jar, rattling the keys. The sound was grating. "The game will now begin!" she announced. She placed the mason jar in the bag and moved it aside.

With a dainty flick of her wrist, Joselle chose one of the small bottles. She unscrewed the tarnished metal top and rubbed a generous amount of some of the clear golden liquid on her arm. She replaced the bottle and chose another one. This one was filled with a cloudy liquid tinted a suspiciously bright blue color. Joselle leaned over toward Blaze and splashed his shirt with it. She was so close that Blaze could practically taste the perfume she was wearing. It was overpowering and sweet.

"Now smell yourself," Joselle instructed.

Blaze did as he was told.

"That is your personal scent. Now you have to become a different person—someone who would smell like that."

Blaze was confused. His face was blank. "I don't get it," he said, mindful of Joselle's delight and discouraged that he didn't understand.

"Watch and learn," Joselle said. She sniffed her arm. "This is a beautiful, flowery perfume," she commented, her eyes half closed. She sniffed her arm again, then inhaled and exhaled luxuriantly. "I am definitely a Veronica," she said, speaking with a lilting accent. "Veronica Marsdale. And I am someone's perfect mother. Picture me wearing a carnation pink dress and lipstick that's thick and cakey in a nice way." She leaned toward Blaze again and whispered into his ear. "Who are you?" she asked, still speaking as Veronica.

Now Blaze understood how to play, but it took him a minute to come up with something. He fidgeted with his hair while he thought. The bright blue liquid was a dreadfully spicy after-shave. "I am Bruno Slobkin," he finally said in his deepest voice, flexing his muscles. He smiled to himself at this notion.

"Ha!" Joselle screeched. "That's good! That is really good."

That afternoon, shaded beneath the black locust tree, Joselle, Keeper of the Scents, rubbed and sprayed Blaze and herself with various perfumes, colognes, and after-shaves. They even used leaves, dirt, and berries. And depending on the particular mixture of smells, they became different people: famous movie stars, characters from books, or simply people they made up themselves.

Blaze laughed until his side ached and he had to massage it. He could not remember when he had laughed so hard.

Periodically throughout their game, Joselle—hand in mouth—would hum theme songs from television programs and make Blaze guess what they were.

"Why are you pretending to play music on your teeth?" Blaze asked, after successfully naming a tune.

"Because my teeth are as big as piano keys," Joselle said. "And it's a special talent."

"How long have you been doing this?" he asked in his Bruno Slobkin voice.

"Since the very day I was born, sweetheart," she answered, speaking with a pronounced southern accent.

During a particularly quiet moment when Blaze was trying to come up with the name of a song, he almost told Joselle about the words of stone. But he stopped himself for some reason. He just couldn't force the words out.

After they had been playing for quite some time, Joselle asked suddenly, "Can I come over to your house?"

"I don't know," said Blaze. The growing effect of their concoctions was light-headedness. He experienced a fluttering in his stomach, too. "I'd have to ask my grandma first." He stared at his knees. "And my dad. Maybe tomorrow would be better, or something."

"Then come over to mine," said Joselle. "You can call your grandma to let her know where you are." She gathered her belongings into her paper sack, her little bottles falling together and clinking against the mason jar.

Blood beat in Blaze's ears. He watched her get up and start to walk away.

"Come on," said Joselle. "Are you part statue?"

"I can't go," he said.

"Why?"

The way she said it, and the way she looked at him, made him feel invisible. "I'm afraid of your grandma's dog," he admitted shyly.

"Gary?" Joselle's eyes widened and she stretched her mouth in an exaggerated fashion. *"Gary?"*

"He's so big. And sometimes at night I can hear him bark all the way over at my house."

Joselle approached him and grabbed his arm as if she were going to pull him down the hill behind her. She clucked her tongue. "Silly," she said. Then she looked right at him, and as she did, Blaze saw something register in her eyes, and he felt something change in her grip. "You're *really* afraid of him, aren't you?" she asked, her voice serious and quiet.

Blaze nodded.

"Don't worry. Gary's just a pussycat. I'll introduce you properly and teach you to like each other. He smells awful, but that's his only bad point. And we don't smell so great, either. He'll like you."

"Really?"

"I promise," she said, waving him along. "What are friends for?"

JOSELLE

Something was shifting and changing inside Joselle. It didn't happen all of a sudden, but gradually, over the course of long, hot summer days. It was a feeling she couldn't exactly describe, except to say that it was private and dense and tight. She felt as if she owned something wonderful that no one else in the whole world knew about. She first became aware of the feeling the afternoon she taught Blaze how to pet Gary.

"I can't do this," Blaze had said, backing away.

"Yes, you can," Joselle told him.

Gary romped forward, pulling his chain taut, his tail wagging fast and hard.

Joselle petted Gary and commanded him to sit. Then

she stood behind Blaze and slowly pushed him toward Gary. She could feel him shake. "Stay," she said to Gary. "Now give me your hand, Blaze." She guided his hand, gently forcing it along the back of Gary's coarse head, again and again.

Blaze made a small sound in his throat.

"See, it's easy."

"Kind of," Blaze said.

Joselle suspected that it wasn't easy at all for Blaze, and she moved her hand with his like a shadow, nudging it along when he hesitated. And as she did, something occurred to her. He needs me, she thought. Blaze Werla needs me.

The following day the feeling washed over her again. She was showing Blaze the spoon trick. They were on the hill.

"I don't believe it," Blaze said, excited.

"It works every time," said Joselle. "Really, truly. Give it a try."

Blaze took the spoon from Joselle and moved it in front of his face. Closer, closer, farther away. Then he turned the spoon over and moved it again. "I'm always upside down on the inside," he commented. "And right side up on the outside."

Joselle nodded thoughtfully. "I told you. It's one of the small wonders of the world." And that's when the feeling struck. Watching the expression on Blaze's face, Joselle thought she knew how teachers must feel after they've successfully explained the mystery of long division.

A few days later, Joselle experienced the feeling under completely different circumstances. She wasn't helping anyone; she was being waited on by Blaze and Nova. She had been invited to Blaze's house for lunch. She was so impressed by the smells of fresh-baked bread and homemade cookies, by the matching towels with rickrack trim, by the flowers in coffee tins lined up on the counter, that afterward she couldn't even remember what day it was, and she actually danced around the table and offered to wash the dishes.

Perhaps it was Nova's bread that had done Joselle in. It was absolutely wonderful. Vicki and Floy were both partial to store-bought bread, the bleached white kind that is so puffed up with air and preservatives that it looks and smells like something kindergarteners are given to express themselves creatively. Occasionally Joselle would form little balls with her bread, and using the dull, knobby ends of the silverware, shoot them around the kitchen table billiard-style.

"You elevate the concept of playing with your food to new heights," one of Vicki's boyfriends had commented once.

"It's better than eating it," Joselle had replied, striking a cereal bowl with a small grayish wad.

One afternoon after she had eaten several meals and snacks at Blaze's house, Joselle asked Nova, "When was the last time you bought bread at a store?"

"I can't remember," Nova answered. "Baking bread is a cinch—and it's one of life's greatest pleasures," she added, smiling.

"I help with the kneading sometimes," Blaze said.

"You don't buy frozen or canned vegetables, either, do you?" Joselle asked.

"Not usually," Nova replied. "I freeze and can myself. Why?"

"Just checking," Joselle said, spreading butter on a slice of warm whole wheat. She licked her fingers, feeling drunk.

The feeling came back to Joselle even when she didn't expect it, even when she was alone. She wondered if she was falling in love with Blaze and his family. Was that possible?

She still experienced what she called "the hollow feeling" or "the Sunday afternoon feeling," but it seemed to come less often. She associated the feeling with The Beautiful Vicki.

Joselle used to think that she would end up alone. A spinster. Not a timid, frail woman with blue hair and lacy dresses, but a feisty woman who wore young, stylish clothes. A woman who could take care of herself. But now she wasn't so certain. Maybe living in a family could really work.

Sometimes Joselle tried to see herself through Blaze's eyes. Depending on her mood, she would see a fat, loud girl who, strangely, played music on her teeth. Or a strong, beautiful girl capable of mesmerizing boys and their families.

□   □   □

Each morning Joselle awaited the arrival of the mail. And each morning she was disappointed. She'd run to the mailbox at the edge of the road as soon as the red, white, and blue truck puttered away. With her eyes closed, she'd open the mailbox and reach into the dark space greedily. Without fail, her hope quickly disappeared; there was never anything addressed to her. After slamming the mailbox shut, she'd kick dirt all the way back to the house, and then toss the bills, letters, and advertisements for Floy carelessly on the kitchen table. She cursed her mother under her breath. The Beautiful Vicki hadn't sent even one postcard. She hadn't telephoned again, either. If Joselle thought about her mother long enough, she became so worked up she was convinced that her bones would twist out of their sockets and snap into sharp pieces.

"I didn't get anything from her either," said Floy one morning when Joselle looked especially disappointed.

"Well, you're not her daughter," Joselle said testily, pulling her chin.

"I'm her mother."

"That's different," Joselle said. She made a paper airplane out of a ShopKo circular. The lines of her folds and creases were precise as cut glass. "Maybe it's your fault she is the way she is," Joselle said, giving Floy a challenging look. Joselle sent the plane toward the garbage pail in a perfect arc, but it careened off course at the last minute and landed in Gary's water dish. Joselle pretended that the plane was an arrow and that the water dish was her mother's black heart.

"Try not to worry about your mother too much," Floy said softly, drumming her fingers on the counter. "She has the annoying habit of being happiest when those who love her the most are upset."

Floy's words confused Joselle, and she tried to make sense of them as she ran over to Blaze's house. She knocked fiercely on the door.

"Hi," said Blaze through the screen, looking gauzy. "What do you want to do today?"

Joselle pulled the door open a crack and squeezed inside. "It doesn't matter," she replied.

And it didn't. She just wanted to be there.

□   □   □

They began spending more and more time together. And when they parted at dusk, Joselle eagerly awaited morning when they would join one another again—usually on the hill.

Sometimes Joselle called him The Boy with the Apricot Hair. And sometimes she called him Blazey. But mostly she called him Blaze.

Sometimes Joselle wanted to tell Blaze everything about her life. But she didn't. She held back. What if he didn't like what he heard? What if he found out that she had written the words on the hill with stones? She had

no idea how he had reacted to them—except that someone had always dismantled them. Would he still want to
be her friend?

Sometimes Joselle wanted to know everything about
Blaze's life. But she decided not to ask too many questions. She fabricated what she didn't know. And the history and circumstances she invented for him were exactly
what she wanted them to be.

Sometimes Joselle liked to be alone with Blaze on the
hill—playing with the hot, hot sun beating down on
them, or sitting quietly against the black locust tree like
bookends in the cool shade. And sometimes she liked to
be with his entire family at their sturdy, round kitchen
table. Blaze and Nova and Glenn and Claire.

Sometimes Joselle wished she could live with them.
Sometimes she wished she were Blaze.

17
JOSELLE

"Ha!" Joselle shouted, storming into Blaze's bedroom, taking him by surprise. She was struck enough by Blaze's expression to add, "It's okay. I didn't mean to scare you." She joined him on the braided rug, plopping down so heavily that the walls seemed to vibrate. Although Joselle had spent a fair amount of time at Blaze's house, she had never been in his room before. She looked around, collecting details and storing them away. "Your grandma let me in. She told me I could come up here. Second door on the right."

Blaze seemed particularly quiet. His cheeks reddened

as he abruptly scooped up the toy he was playing with. "Let me just put this away," he said, talking so fast that Joselle had to decode his words, taking a few moments to understand him.

"What have you got?" Joselle asked, reaching around Blaze's arm and picking up a handful of small plastic animals. A camel, a swan, a goat.

"It's this stupid old toy I used to play with," Blaze replied. "I was just looking at it."

"It's a Noah's ark," Joselle announced. Without asking, she grabbed the toy out of Blaze's hands and scrutinized it. "I hate to tell you this, but it's defective—there are supposed to be two of every animal and you've just got one."

Blaze only nodded.

"Well, it fits, doesn't it? It's a Noah's ark for orphans." Joselle broke down completely with spasms of laughter, holding her belly with both hands. She quieted down quickly, however, since Blaze only averted his eyes and remained silent. Not even a flicker of a smile touched his lips. "I was trying to be funny, but I guess I'm about as funny as a big fat cinder block." She handed the ark back to Blaze and began picking at the cuticle of her thumb. "Sorry. Really," she said as gently as possible, offering the words as a gift.

Today is turning out to be a bad day, Joselle thought. First, no postcard from The Beautiful Vicki. Again. Then, I took it out on Grammy. Again. And now Blaze thinks I'm a dope. I shouldn't have joked about being an orphan. And I never should have lied about my father being dead in the first place.

She was sorry about that, but in a sense he *was* dead. At least to her. If she told Blaze the truth now, he'd hate her for sure. And that wasn't what she wanted at all. She wanted to be friends with Blaze Werla. Very best friends.

How many lies had she told Blaze? It was hard to keep track of them all. She had lied about her father. Lied about her mother being a scientist. She had lied about when she had arrived at her grandmother's house, so that Blaze wouldn't think she had had anything to do with the words of stone. And the words of stone were a kind of lie, too. She wished she had never written them.

Blaze had been the perfect candidate for deceit, and Joselle had gladly taken advantage of his innocence. Pin-pricks of regret ran up and down her legs. No more lies, she told herself. No more words of stone. Joselle made a promise to herself never to lie again. She vowed to be honest in every way until the day she died, or as long as she possibly could. Which wasn't very long. Because as soon as Blaze's back was turned, Joselle sneaked the tiny plastic fox that Blaze had overlooked from beside his dresser and slipped it into her pocket. She couldn't stop herself. *This* is the last dishonest thing I will ever do, she said to herself. Ever, ever, ever.

After shoving the ark under his bed, Blaze pulled his

bedspread down until it touched the floor, hiding the ark entirely. He appeared to be more relaxed now. "I can't play with you today," he said. "I've got to go with my dad and Claire."

"Where?"

"Claire is selling her artwork at a fair. My dad and I are going to help her."

"Can I come, too? Please? If I'm there it'll be more fun."

Blaze seemed to blossom. "Let's ask," he said, already out the door and in the hallway.

The stairs sounded hollow as Joselle pounded down them. She caught up to Blaze and nearly knocked him over, she was moving so fast. She extended her left arm, placing her hand on his shoulder to stop herself. Her right hand was in her front pocket, her fingers wound tightly around the tiny fox. The fox was nearly weightless, but felt heavy against her leg.

□ □ □

From the instant Joselle slid into the van with Glenn, Claire, and Blaze, she pretended that they were her father, mother, and brother. Buckled safely into her seat, she watched them fondly. She studied Glenn first, deciding quickly that she approved of every part that formed her new father. Longish blond hair, big hands, thick wrists, scratchy voice. How are you supposed to feel about a father? she wondered. Or a brother, for that matter?

She knew a bit more about mothers. But Claire seemed very different from Vicki. Vicki was surely beautiful; she worked hard at it with lipstick and eyeliner and curlers and manicures and hair spray. Claire didn't appear to be wearing any makeup, and her hair was simply pulled back into a ponytail with a red rubber band. But she looked beautiful, too. Her features were larger than Vicki's, but more stately, as though she belonged in a painting hanging in a museum in Paris. The Beautiful Vicki would be more at home on the cover of *Cosmopolitan*.

Joselle loosened her seat belt slightly and leaned forward, her chin resting against the front seat. This is my perfect family, she said to herself. When Joselle closed her eyes, she saw them (herself included) etched onto the backs of her eyelids. An aerial view. The four of them formed a rectangle that crept along the highway slowly and silently like a small toy. She basked in her newfound feeling of belonging all the way to the art fair.

Claire had rented the van because she needed room for her artwork and her display booth. Neither her car nor Glenn's would suffice. The van was silvery gray, and Joselle imagined that it was a sleek limousine taking them to a very important private party.

Claire was driving, but Glenn helped to check for traffic as they veered into the parking lot. When he turned his head from side to side, Joselle noticed the circular birthmark on the back of his neck. "One world," she said aloud, wanting to touch the birthmark with her finger.

"What?" asked Blaze.

"Oh, nothing," said Joselle, blushing. "I was just talking to myself."

Joselle and Blaze helped Claire and Glenn set up the display. Glenn and Claire did most of the work. Joselle tried to look busy, but she couldn't keep herself from holding her head high and gazing about loftily at the people who passed by. They all just assume that we're a family, she thought happily.

Joselle didn't know very much about art, but in her opinion Claire's work was exquisite. Claire was selling pins, barrettes, and a few of her boxes. Everything was gold, silver, bronze—and glinting. Claire's work made Joselle think of royalty and perfection and miniature heirlooms people tuck away in secret places that aren't found until years later.

A particular barrette shaped like a fleur-de-lis caught Joselle's attention. She looked at it longingly. She pictured her hair swept back off her face and fastened by the shiny golden swirls. She pictured strangers stopping to get a better look, transfixed by her beauty.

"Come on," Blaze said, tugging on Joselle's sleeve. "Let's go spend the money my dad gave us for lunch."

There was so much to choose from. They bought hot

dogs, soda, popcorn, and—best of all—cotton candy, whipped and spun onto paper cones like fancy pink hairdos. Joselle loved how cotton candy melted when it touched her tongue. She ate hers and nearly half of Blaze's. Her teeth ached from all the sugar.

"This is fun," Blaze said.

"Yeah," said Joselle. "But I think I ate too much."

They were seated at a picnic table, among many, under a large yellow tent. The sunlight shone through the tent, casting a jaundiced look onto everything.

"Want to walk around?" Blaze asked.

"Let's just sit a while longer," Joselle said. "We can watch people."

"Okay."

Joselle played with the soggy paper cone from her cotton candy. "Did you ever wish you were someone else?" she asked.

Blaze shrugged. "Not really."

"I do, sometimes." Joselle waited for Blaze to ask: who? But when he didn't, she continued. "Is there anything about yourself you'd change if you could? Is there anything you don't like?"

Blaze shrugged again.

"I'd get rid of these awful teeth, if I could." Joselle said, pointing to her mouth. "And I'd like to be smaller. Like you."

"I wish I was *bigger*," Blaze said. "And I don't like my scars. From the fire."

Joselle played dumb. "What scars?"

110

Blaze got off the bench and walked over to Joselle's side of the picnic table. "These," he said, turning his ankles and nodding. "I was in a fire one Fourth of July. I got burned—so did three other kids. It wasn't *that* bad. They did some skin grafting. I think they could do more if I really wanted them to. . . ."

Joselle leaned over and touched Blaze's right ankle. "They're tiny," she said. "I'd take your scars over my teeth any day. I always wanted a scar. They make you look brave."

"Really?"

Joselle nodded. "Yeah."

"You wouldn't lie to me?" said Blaze.

"Never," Joselle replied, feeling her cheeks turn pink as polished apples. "Let's go," she said, rising abruptly from the bench and running toward the crowd.

"Wait up," Blaze called.

They wove in and out of the artists' booths. Sometimes Joselle ran ahead and hid behind a tree or a group of people, then rushed out in front of Blaze. Small red flags flapped in the breeze.

"Look!" Joselle said suddenly, bending over. "A lucky penny."

"Let's see," said Blaze.

Joselle handed the penny to Blaze. "It's yours," she said, "on one condition. You have to tell me your wish."

Blaze's little fingers curled and uncurled around the penny. "Right now?"

"Think about it and let me know. But if you don't

111

tell me, it won't come true. True, true, true," Joselle called, running ahead again, dodging in and out of the crowd.

□   □   □

Throughout the afternoon, Joselle was content to sit and observe. She watched Claire interact with the shoppers and browsers. And she watched Glenn holding Claire's money box, making change when he needed to. But when she and Blaze went back to the refreshment stand to get something for Glenn and Claire to eat, Joselle did more than observe. When a boisterous man cut ahead of Blaze in line, Joselle elbowed him. "Excuse me!" she said crisply. "My friend was here first." She felt very protective.

It wasn't until they were driving home at sunset that Joselle remembered that she had taken the fox from Blaze's room. And it dawned on her why she had done it. With the fox in her possession, she might have a kind of power over Blaze. It might add strength to her wishes concerning him. Unlike the key collection he had given her, the fox's whereabouts were unknown to him; that's why it was powerful. The fox represented her secret life with Blaze's family, the life that played out in her head.

There were occasional periods of silence as they rode. But they weren't awkward. They were breaks in the conversation in which time stood still, in which everything

112

was suspended except Joselle's watchful eye. Even so, the ride was going much too quickly for Joselle. She wanted this day to last.

It was Blaze who broke a particularly long silence as they neared Floy's house. "Here," Blaze whispered, his voice as quiet as insects' wings. "You found this. It really belongs to you." He gave Joselle the lucky penny. "And you don't even have to tell me what your wish is."

The penny floated on the sweaty creases of Joselle's palm. She was touched. She pushed the penny into her pocket with the fox. Then she opened her mouth and tapped out "When You Wish Upon a Star." Her fingers smelled metallic.

Blaze joined in on his own teeth. They played it together, smiling, until the van pulled up to Floy's front porch.

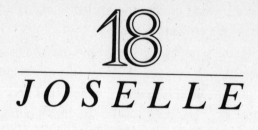

JOSELLE

"**H**ow was your day?" Floy asked, head poised, waiting. She had been leafing through a magazine. It lay open on her lap.

"It was the best day of my life," Joselle said. She flung herself onto the sofa, her arms spread out over her head like a giant V. She sighed dreamily.

"I'm glad you had a good time," Floy said. "Tell me about it."

Joselle lay motionless on the sofa. She couldn't tell Floy. If she did, wouldn't Floy feel terrible? Wouldn't it bother her that her granddaughter could have more fun with someone else's family than she ever could with her own? "I can't exactly explain it," Joselle said finally. "I

114

mean, it wasn't *that* great. It was okay." Her lip flickered. She forced a laugh and got up to go to the bathroom. "I've had better days. For sure."

Floy closed her magazine. "I can't keep up with your
thoughts," she said.

◻   ◻   ◻

In Joselle's dream the moon was blue. And then it
became a penny. And then it vanished. She sat up in the
middle of the night with Blaze's words on the tip of her
tongue: "You wouldn't lie to me?" And her answer
haunted her: "Never."

She rose from the sofa and walked to the front window. There was no moon. It was raining. Water
streamed down the window as though she were under
the sea. She felt regretful. Joselle pulled her purse out
from beneath the sofa. She searched for her four-color
pen.

While the slow steady rain tap-tap-tapped against the
house, Joselle darkened the ball-point-pen tattoos on her
thigh. When they faded, she would darken them again.
She would keep them as a reminder. She would keep
them until she told Blaze the truth.

About everything.

The words of stone.

Her father.

Her mother.

The tiny fox.

Joselle placed the lucky penny under her pillow. She wished that when she told Blaze the truth, he would forgive her. She wished that she had a million lucky pennies; she felt she needed that much luck.

◻   ◻   ◻

When Joselle woke up again, it was still raining. She put on her bikini and ran up and down the front sidewalk several times. The rain chilled her, and goose bumps sprouted on her arms and legs. But she felt much better, exhilarated.

She came inside, toweled off, and wrapped herself around a steaming cup of tea. Floy's door was still closed to the morning, so Joselle was very quiet. She wanted to get out of the house before Floy got up. She pulled her extra-large white T-shirt on over her damp bikini. The shirt fell to her knees, covering the tattoos easily. She wore her new sweater, her dangly rhinestone earrings, her red rubber thongs. She brushed her hair back into a ponytail as Claire had done yesterday. Joselle's ponytail wasn't nearly as long as Claire's, but she thought it looked smart, and with her hair away from her face, her earrings were more visible. She left a note for Floy by the coffeepot.

Puddles dotted Floy's lawn like scattered mirrors. But Joselle didn't mind. She hopped off the porch and skipped across the soggy yard toward Blaze's house, her feet sliding in and out of her thongs. Floy's umbrella shielded her like an enormous lavender flower.

She didn't feel brave enough today to tell the truth. She just wanted to see her friend.

BLAZE

The steely smell of rain was in the morning air. Blaze liked rainy days. "That's the artist in you," Nova said time and time again. "Most creative people like gray weather." Blaze didn't know if that was true, but he knew that Glenn also liked dark, stormy days. And according to Glenn, Reena had felt exactly the same way.

Reena hadn't been a painter, but a writer. She had majored in English in college. Before Blaze was born, she had taken a job with the local newspaper, writing book reviews. After Blaze was born, she stayed home with him, hoping to write a novel one day. Glenn said that Reena was never satisfied with her attempts at a novel and therefore had never kept any of them. Some-

118

times Blaze pretended that his mother *had* written a book. A book that could be checked out at the library. A book with secret references to him.

Blaze's train of thought was broken by a series of loud knocks on the door.

It was Joselle. She smiled radiantly and waved at Blaze, then flew off the porch into the rain. Instead of holding her umbrella above her, she swung it around, turning circles with it, dancing. She raced about like a top—spinning, twirling, laughing.

"Come out!" she yelled, waving. "It's fun!"

Blaze opened the door and stepped onto the porch. It was pouring. He could see that Joselle was soaked already. He could see her bathing suit beneath her T-shirt and sweater.

"Come on!" she shouted.

Blaze hesitated, thinking. It was only a summer shower. Nova wouldn't mind. He took off his shoes and sprang from the porch, cringing from the shivery rain. He joined Joselle in a large muddy puddle.

Joselle put her umbrella down and grabbed Blaze's hands, pulling him into her dance. "I'm drenched," she said, giggling, kicking her leg out playfully.

And then he saw it. His mother's name written on Joselle's thigh. He could see it through her wet, wet T-shirt which was plastered against her skin. And he could see parts of other words. All the words of stone curving around her leg in ink of various colors.

Blaze jerked his hands out of hers harshly. They stood face to face.

"What's wrong?" Joselle asked.

"I want my key collection back," Blaze said between quick, shallow breaths, his voice shaking with anger. It was all he could think of to say.

Joselle didn't answer, her face uncomprehending. Blaze could feel the silence in his belly.

Holding his breath, Blaze tried to calm himself. He squinted and concentrated, his eyelashes becoming veils that filtered things and blurred them. But it did little good; he just kept seeing the words of stone as they had appeared on the hill. He felt ashamed for being such an easy target, someone so easily tricked.

"You wrote the messages on the hill, didn't you?" he asked. "You wrote my mother's name."

"Oh!" Joselle said, glancing down at her transparent shirt, understanding. She covered the words with her hands and pulled her legs together. "No. I mean . . . yes." She looked away. "I'm sorry," she said. "It was just a joke. I didn't mean anything bad by it. And I stopped doing it once I got to know you." She knitted her fingers nervously. "Really."

"I thought you were my friend," Blaze said. His voice cracked. His fingers were extended on both hands like the points of stars. They whirled around his legs as he spoke. "Just get out of here." He gave her a hard mean look.

"You don't like me anymore," Joselle whispered, turning sideways, hiding her face. "I'm *sorry*," she reminded him, turning back, flipping a loose piece of hair out of her eyes. She still didn't look at him directly. "Please, don't hate me."

For a fraction of a second everything became razor sharp to Blaze. The pores on Joselle's face, the liquid of her eyes, each strand of hair, each drop of rain. Everything was so clearly defined that it hurt Blaze's eyes to rest them on anything.

In that instant, Blaze rushed toward Joselle and pushed her down as hard as he could. He hit her once across her shoulders. "Get out of here," he said. "Just get out of here." And then he grabbed one of the round buttons on her sweater and pulled it off, thread trailing behind it like a fine tail.

He didn't see her face again. He watched as she rose from the ground, picked up her umbrella, and scrambled across the driveway toward Floy's house without looking back. And that's when he started to cry.

□   □   □

By early afternoon the rain had passed and the sun was shining. Birds chirped and skittered through the ribbons of water in Nova's garden. Barefooted and shirtless, Blaze spent the rest of the day tagging along behind his grandmother while she weeded, or sitting by

121

himself in small spaces: his closet, under the porch, between a pile of bricks and the outside wall of Glenn's
studio.

"You seem to be miles from here," Nova said, cocking
her head so Blaze could hear her. "Are you feeling all
right?"

"I'm fine," Blaze replied, gazing at a clump of nastur-
tiums until it became the sun.

Alone, resting against Glenn's studio wall, it occurred
to Blaze that he had never pushed anyone the way he
had pushed Joselle. He had never hit anyone, either. Or
purposely ruined something that belonged to someone
else. The button from Joselle's sweater reminded him of
what he had done. Perhaps it always would.

But no one had ever made him feel so stupid before.
No one had ever humiliated him the way Joselle had.
No one had ever been so mean. He couldn't believe she
had done it. And he couldn't believe that he had accused
Claire in his mind.

He wished that he hadn't shown Joselle his scars. And
he shuddered to think that he had nearly confided in her
about the words of stone.

Now he felt as though he should have known. But how
could he have known? Joselle had lied about when she
had arrived at her grandmother's house. And when he
had met her on the hill, she had told him that she had
never been on the hill before. She'd probably lied a million times, he thought.

Or was there a part of him that suspected Joselle all along? If there had been, he just kept pushing it deeper and deeper inside himself until it virtually vanished. He had wanted to like her so much.

During the past couple weeks, Blaze had started to feel as though he had been friends with Joselle forever, but now he didn't know what was true. He didn't know what to believe.

Sitting alone, Blaze realized something else: he hadn't thought of Simon in days. Had Joselle taken his place?

Between his fingers, the button was as smooth as candy. He put it in his mouth and sucked on it.

20

JOSELLE

"I hate you," Joselle said to her reflection in the living room window. "I hate you, I hate you, I hate you." When she turned off the lamp on the end table, her reflection disappeared and everything was dark. Joselle remained by the window; it was past midnight, but she knew it was useless to try to fall asleep. By now she was beyond the point of crying. After dinner, in the bathtub, she had cried so much that her eyes were swollen and raw. So was her thigh. She had scrubbed the ball-point-pen tattoos with a vengeance so that the few remaining lines were as faint as thin spidery veins. "I hate you," she repeated. Joselle pinched her arm right above her wrist until she couldn't stand it any longer and there were red dents from her fingernails in her skin.

She felt the way she did at school when she hadn't prepared for a test, only much worse. An overwhelming sense of panic and frustration would fill her head like a storm, making it nearly impossible to sit still at her desk. What was the best thing to do? she'd always wonder. Guess, and most likely answer the questions incorrectly? Or leave the lined answer spaces empty? She'd weigh the odds in her mind, nearly always opting for leaving the test completely blank except for her name—which she would spend most of the period working on, carefully printing each letter with decorative touches. That made things for her teachers more complex, more baffling. Most of her teachers regarded her with suspicion and wrinkled noses, as if she were some kind of specimen that was hard to categorize.

Once, when she had completely forgotten about a vocabulary test for Mrs. Weynand's language arts class, Joselle felt compelled to approach Mrs. Weynand with a sincere hug and explain how awful she felt. But she knew that that would never work; there was too much history between them for Mrs. Weynand ever to think of Joselle as anything but trouble. A constant inconvenience.

But this wasn't a test in school. This was more important.

Joselle needed someone to talk to. She hadn't told Floy about what had happened at Blaze's house, because Floy's patience was wearing thin. Upon seeing the wet, dirtied cashmere sweater—twigs and weeds sprouting

from the sleeves—Floy threw her arms up in exasperation. Her eyeballs rolled back and her mouth popped
open like a fish when she noticed the missing button.
"You'll never be able to match that pretty button," she
said, yanking the sweater toward her to get a better look
and releasing it with a snap, as though a mannequin
were wearing it, not a person. "I'm not even going
to ask what you've been up to. Just get yourself show-
ered and cleaned and dried. And give me the
sweater," Floy added. "I'll try to fix it up." Then she
sighed heavily and shook her head. Joselle knew that
she was fast becoming the same person in her grandmother's eyes that she was in the eyes of her teachers.
Anyway, Floy was surely asleep by now. And Gary
was little consolation.

Joselle needed her mother.

On the end table, resting against the lamp, stood a
framed photograph of Joselle, Vicki, Floy, and Floy's
mother, Alice. The photo was taken in the hospital on
the day that Joselle was born. "Four Generations of
Women," Joselle had called the photograph once. "I'd
call it 'Four Generations of Fighting and Headaches,'"
Vicki had retorted. Joselle thought it was odd that she
had such a vivid memory when it came to Vicki's hurtful
comments. She shrugged to herself.

Although Joselle's great-grandmother Alice died before Joselle had formed a memory of her, Joselle sensed
a strong connection to her. In the photograph Alice's

heart-shaped face was a lacework of grooves; Vicki's was flushed and young. Floy appeared stern and uneasy, and Joselle was a chubby bundle the color of a bruise. It was too dark to see the photograph clearly, but Joselle knew it like she knew the image of George Washington on a dollar bill.

The only information that Joselle had about her great-grandmother was from photographs and from stories Vicki and Floy had told her. When she was younger, Joselle had thought of Alice as a guardian angel, a bent, wrinkled woman who lived inside the crack in Joselle's bedroom ceiling. Someone who was able to see and know all things. Someone who would emerge upon request to rescue and comfort Joselle. As routine, Joselle used to say good-night and good morning to the crack every day. It didn't take Joselle very long, however, to come to the conclusion that the crack was only damaged plaster and that her great-grandmother could never, ever truly help her.

Once, when Joselle lost one of Vicki's favorite earrings and was sent to her room as punishment, Joselle called for Alice. "Here, Alice! Here, Old Grammy!" she cried. At first she waited patiently, sitting cross-legged on her bed, her head tilted upward. When Alice failed to respond, Joselle climbed onto her dresser and removed the curtain rod from the window frame. Using the curtain rod as a tool, she chipped away at the ceiling until bits of plaster dusted her bedspread like snow and she knew in the very bottom of her heart that what she was doing was not only pointless, but would only get her into more trouble.

□   □   □

In the moonlight Joselle wandered. From room to room she roamed without purpose. After she had walked through every room (except Floy's bedroom) several times, Joselle found herself back in the living room beside Floy's rocking chair, staring down at the telephone. With the telephone cord spiraled around her, Joselle dialed her own number. She wanted Vicki to magically answer the phone and say: "Hello, sweetie! Of course it's me. I'm having all the calls forwarded to me in California. Whatever it is you want, I'll do. I'll be on the next plane home if you need me." But all she heard was the faraway sound of a dull bell in an empty house. Joselle let the phone ring and ring and ring. She pictured her mother and Rick running along the beach, the or-ange-and-pink sun dropping into the Pacific Ocean be-hind them. She pulled the cord across her face, placed it in her mouth, wove it between her fingers. She was all set to hang up, when suddenly she heard a sleepy, but familiar, voice bark, "Hello? *Hello?* Who *is* this?"

Joselle hung up the phone without saying anything. She fell into the rocking chair. After the initial shock passed, she cried in rhythm with the movement. Back, forth. Whimper, sniffle. She cried quietly at first, like someone at a movie. But then she began to rock faster and cry louder. When she thought that she might completely lose control, she sprang from the chair and barged into Floy's room.

"Grammy," she sobbed. "Grammy, help."

21

JOSELLE

While Floy talked on the telephone, Joselle sat on the floor behind the sofa. The longer Floy talked, the louder her voice grew. "I don't care if it *is* one o'clock in the morning," Floy said. "What are *you* doing home? Your daughter and I were led to believe that you and your friend were somewhere out west."

Twisting this way and that way, Joselle tried to hear better, tried not to hear, tried to see Floy's expression, tried to hide her own eyes so she couldn't see a thing. Joselle heard Floy say, "What do you *mean*, you've been home all along?" and "I don't care what you call it, I call it lying," and "Too bad the word responsibility isn't in your vocabulary," and "You'll never change," and "Nothing's ever your fault, is it?"

By the time Floy slammed the receiver down, she was shouting. Her "Good-bye!" made Joselle cringe.

"Well," said Floy, her face pinched with anger, "The Beautiful Vicki strikes again. She thinks her wishes are more important than your needs."

Joselle hated talk like this; it meant nothing. She wanted facts. She gave Floy a searching look. "What are we doing?" she cried. "What's *happening*?"

"I'm taking you home where you belong."

"Right now?"

"Right now. I won't be able to sleep. You won't be able to sleep. We might as well." Floy bent down and kissed Joselle on each cheek. "She was home the entire time. The Pacific Ocean thing was just one of her stories." Floy inhaled deeply. So deeply that Joselle thought that Floy might suck in the whole living room. She let out the breath slowly and steadily. "Come here, Joselle," Floy said, her voice changing, turning lighter, almost airy. "Let me do your eyelids one last time."

□   □   □

Within minutes after having her eyelids done, Joselle was packed and they were on the road. Floy was in such a hurry that she and Joselle kept their nightgowns on. Joselle wore a sweatshirt over hers.

Joselle's sweater was lying on a towel on the backseat. It was still wet. Earlier that afternoon, Floy had washed it by hand and sewn on a flat, mismatched, dove-colored button. "It's the best I can do," Floy had told Joselle.

131

When they passed a street lamp, Joselle turned in the car to look at the sweater. It was no longer a perfect thing. It was limp and dull. Now it truly belongs to me, she thought regretfully.

The night was thick and black and full of motion. The white painted lines on the highway slashed through the darkness as if they had been cut with a monstrous knife. There were only a few cars on the road, and when Joselle spotted one she wondered where it was going. She was going home. It may not have been under the best of circumstances, but Joselle Stark was going home.

Joselle's bags were in the trunk, but she kept her purse and her knapsack on the floor between her feet. In the knapsack were her new clothes, the lucky penny, Blaze's key collection, and the fox she had taken from his Noah's ark.

Blaze Werla.

What could she do about him now? Would he ever forgive her? How could she have been so stupid? Why had she danced in the rain?

A small part inside her wanted to forget him—put him out of her life completely, throw his things into the trash when she got home. But she knew that wasn't possible. She had already added him to her life. Most people she trusted ended up breaking her heart into a million pieces. Blaze was different. Why did she have to go and ruin everything?

"I've got something for you," Floy said, interrupting Joselle's thoughts. "Grab the wheel a minute. Traffic's light."

Joselle leaned over and clutched the steering wheel. She turned it ever so slightly, testing it, feeling the power. Floy had never let her do this before and it surprised Joselle. The highway curved gradually and Joselle maneuvered the car expertly.

Floy fished under the seat for a minute and came up with a small, flat bag. "Here it is," she said. She slid the bag onto Joselle's lap and grabbed the wheel, pushing Joselle's hands away. "I bought this the night we went shopping at the mall. I paid for it while you were in the dressing room. I thought I'd keep it and give it to you when you needed it most." Floy flipped the overhead light on.

It was a scarf. A beautiful scarf. It was black, bordered with a network of birds of all kinds, printed in gorgeously bright colors. Every color Joselle knew. And even some she couldn't identify by name.

"Thanks, Grammy. I love it." Joselle stroked one of the birds. "I love you," she told Floy.

"I thought it would look nice with your new sweater. Jazz it up a bit."

A lump formed in Joselle's throat. She wanted to say more to Floy. Apologize for getting the sweater dirty. Thank her again for the scarf. She started to cry.

"I know you don't understand everything your mother does," Floy said. "I don't understand, either. But I know she loves you." Floy rubbed Joselle's knee. "Let's just drive," she said. "Let's just drive and think."

Joselle had a lot to think about. The Beautiful Vicki

topped her list. But if Joselle thought about her mother too long, she was overcome with sadness. She tried to keep the sadness moving. Joselle pictured the inside of her body as a pinball machine. And she willed the sadness—the little steel ball—to stay in motion, moving around and around throughout her. Never stopping. If it stopped, she might explode.

Her mind drifted back to Blaze. He may have been the best friend she ever had. If nothing else, she knew that she had to return the key collection and the tiny fox. It was just a matter of time. Joselle remembered so clearly the night that she had thought of the words of stone, how impressed she had been by her own brilliance. And when she had first looked at Reena's name on the hillside, she had felt so elated that her toes tingled. Thinking about it all now caused her stomach to sink. She had set out to complicate someone else's life, and ended up complicating her own.

And that's when she took her pen from her purse and hiked up her nightgown. I'M SORRY, Joselle wrote on her thigh. And—I'M BACK. And she knew that she would be back. She was counting on it.

Floy glanced over, clicked her tongue, and flicked off the overhead light. "Just drive and think," she said again, softly.

After putting her pen away and readjusting her nightgown, Joselle folded and unfolded the scarf on her lap. Then she wound it loosely around her neck and knotted it above her heart, tossing the ends casually off to the side. Even in the darkness, the birds on the scarf were so colorful, so vivid, that for a brief moment Joselle was certain that she heard them sing. A wild throaty song.

BLAZE

The bedroom simmered with stale heat. Joselle was standing at Blaze's window, looking out toward the hill. She was wearing a skirt that reminded Blaze of a tulip, upside down. The skirt changed color constantly—green to blue to gray. And everything wavered. She was intent, her body firmly fixed to the window frame like a statue. Blaze wanted to see what she was seeing. Was there a message on the hill? He tried to run toward her, but could only move in slow motion, as if he were moving through deep water. By the time he reached the window, Joselle had leaped out. He leaned over the sill, but she was nowhere to be seen. She had disappeared into a blinding yellow light. But her voice came from all around—above, below, and from within. "I'm everywhere," her voice said, echoing in his head like a bell, making his ears ache. "I'm everywhere."

When Blaze woke up, his sheet was pulled over his head, and his room was sizzling with the summer sun.

□   □   □

For days after the incident in the rain, Blaze didn't see Joselle at all. But then he hadn't gone up to the hill since then, and he wasn't exactly sure if he wanted to see her anyway.

He spent a good portion of each day preparing to paint the canvas that Glenn had given him at the start of the summer.

Blaze had decided to try to paint in a manner similar to Glenn's. He would paint a surreal landscape. Blaze knew that people rendered realistically weren't his specialty, so he thought he would choose different objects to represent people he knew. He would have the objects floating in a night sky, stars all around. Anything was possible in the darkest part of the night.

Lying on his bed, Blaze made a list of the people he wanted to include and the objects that might represent them.

> DAD—a paintbrush, his birthmark
> GRANDMA—a cucumber beetle, green
> beans, tomatoes, a flower
> MOM—my ark, the Ferris wheel

Should I include Joselle? he wondered. Or Claire? Or myself?

He added to the list.

JOSELLE (maybe)—a spoon, the button, stones

CLAIRE (maybe)—*long* hair *(not red)*, a silver barrette

ME (maybe)—my key collection, my ark, the Ferris wheel

Some things could stand for more than one person, Blaze realized. A paintbrush could stand for Glenn or himself. Or even Claire, seeing as there were brushes in the box of paints she had given him. His ark and the Ferris wheel could stand for Reena or himself. His key collection also symbolized Joselle, since she had it now. And Joselle's button represented both of them, too; it was hers, but it was in his possession. We're all linked in certain ways, he thought.

He sketched on paper first. While he worked, Blaze remembered the day he had told Joselle that he wanted to be an artist when he was older.

"A famous one?" she asked.

"I don't know," he replied, shrugging. "Just an artist."

"*I'm* going to be famous," Joselle told him, smiling.

"At what?" Blaze asked.

"At whatever I want," Joselle answered. "Currently I plan on being a famous doctor, or at least a surgeon of the heart or brain."

Even though Joselle was on his mind, he decided to concentrate on Glenn and Nova and Reena. Soon, a large paintbrush, green beans, and a tomato circled a full moon. And so did an ark with animals spilling out across the sky.

When Blaze sketched the ark, he set the real one on the floor in front of him. That's when he discovered that his tiny fox was missing. He looked for it under his bed, in his closet, and in all his drawers. I'll find it later, he said to himself.

He worked and reworked his ideas until he was satisfied. Then he smeared charcoal on the back of his drawing, taped it to his canvas, and traced over the drawing. Now the image was on the canvas. He left enough space for other objects he might include later.

With his paints like a box of candy before him, Blaze sat in his room waiting to begin. "Beginning is the hardest part," Glenn always said. Blaze surely felt that now. He waited and waited and waited. He wasn't yet ready to make a mark on the canvas with paint.

□   □   □

The next day Glenn asked Blaze, "Where's Joselle? I haven't seen her around lately."

"I'm not sure," Blaze answered, trying to be as vague as possible.

"Maybe she'd like to come for dinner, too?"

"Oh, not tonight," Blaze said.

"Okay," said Glenn, absently. He was poking at the

fire in the outdoor grill with tongs. Claire was coming for dinner. They were going to have bratwurst.

Blaze was wary of the fire. He stood at a distance and squinted his eyes. He could feel the heat and smell the lighter fluid. Blaze crossed his arms, rubbing his elbows tentatively. His ankles felt itchy. The air above the flames rolled and flickered as though he were looking through waves. It was mesmerizing.

Blaze had asked to invite Claire. It was his way of trying to make up for the times that he had ignored her. Glenn's eyes had glinted when Blaze had suggested it. "Good idea, Blazer," he had said, placing his hand on the back of Blaze's neck and holding it there for a moment.

□   □   □

After dinner, Blaze found a few minutes when he and Claire were alone.

"I wanted you to come for dinner," Blaze told Claire softly. The kitchen table stood between them, a flat brown space. They had already cleared the table of dirty dishes and rinsed them. Water dribbled down Blaze's arm. He wiped it on his pants. "It was my idea."

"I know." Claire's mouth was a perfect circle when she finished saying the word know. And her expression was so bright his head spun.

□   □   □

Before Claire left, she came to Blaze's room to say good-night. The door was open, but she knocked and waited in the hallway.

"You can come in," Blaze said, sitting up. He had been lying on his bed. His Noah's ark was on its side, capsized atop a rumpled mess of bedspread waves. The animals were scattered, adrift among the creases of the sheets. He had been wondering (as he often did) about what happened to all the animals that were left behind, all the animals that weren't allowed into the ark. Did they all drown? And how many animals *had* been left? Hundreds? Thousands? Millions? The waters of the great flood must have stunk, he reasoned. And what about the *people* left behind? That was the worst part about the story of Noah's ark. The part they never really tell you about. What happened to all the people?

"I just wanted to thank you for inviting me tonight," Claire said.

"That's okay," Blaze replied. His cheeks turned hot. "This was my favorite toy when my mother died," he said, picking up the ark and offering it to Claire. Their fingers touched in the exchange.

"It's nice," Claire said. Nodding toward an animal, she said, "May I?"

"Sure." Blaze handed her the tiger. "I had twelve kinds of animals, but just yesterday I realized that my fox is missing. I keep this in the ark to take its place. Until I find the fox." He held up the round, lustrous button from Joselle's sweater.

"No foxes." Claire looked quietly, then gently placed the ark and the tiger at the foot of Blaze's bed. "Well, I should go, but I just wanted to thank you. It was nice to see you again. And thank you for letting me look at your ark. It's an interesting story, don't you think? Mysterious."

Blaze could only nod in agreement. Mysterious was right. He almost pulled his canvas out of his closet to show Claire, but changed his mind.

"Good-night, Blaze," Claire said from the doorway. Her face was in shadow, but her long, ringed fingers waved in the light, catching it and sending it back like miniature comets.

"'Night," he answered. He listened to her oddly rhythmic footsteps pattering down the hallway. She's skipping, he thought, thrilled by the sound and thrilled by the picture it created in his head: a tall adult doing what he had only seen little children and his kindergarten teacher do. Blaze fluffed his pillows and wedged them behind his back. "See you soon," he whispered.

BLAZE

Because he knew he would have to face Joselle sooner or later, Blaze walked up and over the hill to Floy's house and rang the bell. Gary charged for the window and barked so fiercely Blaze shuddered. After a long minute Floy answered the door, opening it just a crack and blocking Gary with her spindly legs.

"Hello, Blaze," she said, her bespectacled nose protruding through the small gap between the door and the doorjamb.

"Hi," he said shyly, trying to keep an eye on Gary. "Can I talk to Joselle?" he asked, twiddling his fingers nervously. "Please?"

"She went back home," Floy replied. "It's been a few

days now. I don't know what Joselle told you, but she was only here for a short visit. For all I know, she told you she moved in here."

Suddenly Blaze felt lonely. "She didn't say good-bye." The boldness of his voice surprised himself.

The door opened wider as Gary quieted down. Blaze could see Floy entirely now. She was wearing a sleeveless white housedress patterned with deep red roses, and she held a magazine in her hand. Her pockets were overflowing with tissues.

Gary slipped past Floy and trotted out onto the porch. He rubbed against Blaze. Blaze scratched Gary behind his ears, trying to remain calm, trying to remember everything Joselle had taught him about dogs. After circling Blaze twice, Gary made himself comfortable in the shady corner of the porch.

"Well, to be truthful," Floy said, "I ended up taking Joselle home in the middle of the night. It was a sudden departure."

"Is Joselle okay?" Blaze had carried the button with him. He felt for it in his pocket and pressed it into his leg. He looked at Floy intensely, seeking an answer.

"Oh, sure. I didn't mean to mislead you. Don't worry about Joselle. She's fine. Joselle's Joselle." Floy swatted at a fly with her magazine. "Listen," she said, "do you want something to eat?" She stepped aside and gestured for Blaze to enter the house. The sweep of her arm pushed the door open all the way. "I think I've got some cookies. Store bought."

"No, thank you," Blaze said politely, moving slowly off the porch. He backed up to the railing and leaned against it. "But—but is she coming back?"

"Oh, she'll be back. As a matter of fact, she ran off at the mouth about you to her mother. She told her mother that she wanted to live here, she liked you so much. Her only true friend in the world, she called you."

Blaze blushed completely and uncontrollably.

"It'd put me away for sure," Floy said. "Having her live with me." She sighed and rolled her eyes. Then her eyes welled. "You know Joselle. She's a handful. But a sweetheart, despite all her troubles." She laughed, and it seemed to Blaze that it wasn't exactly a joyful laugh.

Blaze cleared his throat.

Gary stretched and yawned. A long wheezy yawn followed by heavy panting.

"She really likes you," Floy continued. She was blinking her eyes quickly, as though she had something in them, irritating them. "It's the only time I've ever seen her so interested in another child."

Looking down, Blaze played with his feet, waggling his toes; his shoes seemed sizes too small. "If you talk to her, will you tell her I said hi?"

"I sure will. And you say hello to your father and your grandmother for me. Funny, we live so close and never see each other."

Blaze said that he would. Then he went up to Gary

145

and petted him, cooing to him as he stroked his sides, the way Joselle had shown him. Gary's tail wagged briskly, and Blaze hopped off the porch.

"You're a nice young man," Floy called. "I'd like Joselle to be around you more. Thank you. Thanks a lot."

"Bye," Blaze said, turning back toward Floy for a moment before running home, his heart booming.

He had gone to Floy's with the intention of demanding the return of his key collection, and now he didn't even care about it; he only missed Joselle. He had thought and thought about how he could ever forgive her, and already it was done.

□   □   □

Several mornings later Blaze rose to discover a small wrapped box outside his bedroom door. A note was attached. It said, *I made these for your ark. Love, Claire.*

Blaze opened the package and found a pair of shiny bronze foxes, no larger than an inch in any direction. Blaze picked them up. He hadn't told Claire that he owned only one of each animal. Of course she'd assume there'd be two. The foxes sat on Blaze's palm, heads low, tails curled slightly sidewise. He moved his hand, examining the foxes from every angle. The details fascinated him: delicate lines to indicate fur, the holes that served as eyes, the teensy upturned peaks that formed the pointy noses. The foxes were more sturdy and heavy than Blaze's plastic animals. More beautiful, too.

He looked at the foxes for so long that they became huge. So huge that there was barely enough room in the world for anything else.

□   □   □

Something wasn't right.

Blaze peered at the drawing on his canvas from various distances, tilting his head this way and that way. He still had not begun to paint. He thought of asking Glenn for help, but he wanted to do this all on his own. To make it work.

Blaze had considered adding objects to represent Claire and Joselle to the painting right from the start. And that's exactly what he decided to do.

Claire would be easy. He drew two foxes as expertly as he could, looking carefully at the statues from Claire. He drew them on the underside of the full moon, flying, reaching out and up and toward the ark. The only pair of animals on the canvas.

Joselle was more difficult. But after about an hour of thinking and sketching, it became obvious; with only a few changes, the large, round full moon could also serve as Joselle's button.

It seemed right. Everything circled the button-moon the way Blaze's summer seemed to revolve around Joselle.

He knew it wasn't perfect, but he felt as ready as he would ever be. And so he began to paint.

24
BLAZE

It was August. School would be starting soon. Blaze and Nova were at the cemetery, tending the flowers beside Reena's grave. Glenn had been working with them, but decided to go for a walk. "I'll wait for you by the car," he told them. It was parked at the side of the highway.

"Dad doesn't like it here, does he?" Blaze said. He was pulling handfuls of weeds and piling them into Nova's basket.

"I think he was just ready to leave," Nova said. "It *is* taking me longer than I thought it would, but I wanted to cut all the roses back."

"Sometimes it's scary here," Blaze told her as he watched withering rose petals flutter to the ground.

"Sometimes."

"And sometimes it's just quiet."

"I think you're right."

While Nova finished working with her clippers, Blaze ran his hand over his mother's name. REENA PREHN WERLA. No matter how hot it was outside, the stone felt icy to his touch. The chiseled edges of the letters numbed his fingers. Sometimes he'd press his hand against the stone until an impression was left on his skin. He'd watch it vanish like breath on a window.

When he was in the second grade, Blaze had found a picture of a cemetery in a big book at the school library. He couldn't remember the name of the book, and although he had looked for it again several times, he never found it. The picture was of four boys sitting on tombstones, riding them as if they were horses. The boys were wearing hats and blowing trumpets, as Blaze recalled it. The picture frightened him the day he saw it, and he always thought of it when he came to the cemetery. He could never do what the boys in the picture were doing. But he could imagine Joselle doing it. He saw her clearly. Joselle—hopping onto a gravestone, clicking her heels and whooping, wearing a loopy grin on her face and an outrageous hat on her head. It didn't seem wrong for Joselle.

Blaze took Joselle's button out of his pocket and rolled it along Reena's gravestone. When it fell onto the ground, Blaze picked it up, wiped it off on his shirt, and tucked it into his sock. Sometimes he kept it there, sometimes in his wallet, sometimes in a pocket. But he always carried it with him now, wherever he went.

"We'd better go," Nova said. She leaned on Blaze as she got up.

"It looks nice," Blaze remarked, helping his grandmother gather her things. He felt sleepy all of a sudden, and yawned.

"Give me your hand, Blaze," Nova said. She held it until they reached the car.

□   □   □

Being at the cemetery had given him the idea to go to the hill. He walked around the black locust tree, weaving in and out of the stones.

Blaze thought about the burials he had been responsible for: Benny's, Ajax's, Ken's, Harold's, Ortman's. And everything went fuzzy for a moment. In some ways the whole idea seemed childish to him. Had it always? Or was this some new feeling? He wondered how changes take place in people. He wondered if people knew when things changed in their minds any more than they could feel their bones or hair growing.

Blaze took the five stones, added one for Simon, and formed a letter *J* with them as best he could near the black locust tree.

He hadn't seen Joselle since the morning in the rain.

He wondered if he'd ever see her again.

150

□   □   □

When Blaze painted, hours could pass without his knowing, and he could vacillate between complete satisfaction with his work and total disappointment within that time over and over again.

It had taken Blaze weeks to finish the canvas. He had gotten to the point where he just couldn't do anything else to it. And yet, he didn't want to show it to Glenn or Nova or Claire. He didn't want to explain what anything meant.

Blaze signed his name in the lower right-hand corner of the canvas, using little white dots of paint to form the letters.

□   □   □

On the last Saturday in August, Blaze woke up feeling exceptionally buoyant. He and Glenn and Claire were going to the county fair. They would be leaving early and making a day of it. Blaze was out of bed and dressed in minutes. He went to the window and threw open the curtains. The morning was shiny with rain from the night, the air breathtakingly clear. Above the hill, the sky was a radiant blue, and beneath the black locust tree on the slope of the hill were stones. The stones were white moons that bled together. They spelled: I'M SORRY.

Blaze stared at them until all the sounds of the morning quieted to nothing—the birds, the clock, the wind.

Then he pinched himself to verify that he was, in fact, awake and alive, and bounded down the hallway to Glenn's room.

He'd have to explain some things to Glenn, but Blaze felt that he could handle that. There was a lot of telling to do, but he'd only say as much as he needed to for now. Blaze had simply told Glenn and Nova that Joselle had gone home. He hadn't told anyone about the words of stone. Maybe he'd even show Glenn the painting.

Blaze's footsteps were much too loud for early morning, but he didn't seem to notice. He reached Glenn's bedroom and stopped, loosely holding the doorknob. He didn't know where to begin. He thought for a minute, then slowly opened the door.

"Dad," he whispered excitedly, "get up. I want you to look at the hill."

It was a good place to start.